PURRFECT IMPASSE

THE MYSTERIES OF MAX 67

NIC SAINT

PURRFECT IMPASSE

The Mysteries of Max 67

Copyright © 2023 by Nic Saint

All rights reserved. No part of this book may be reproduced in any form by any electronic or mechanical means including photocopying, recording, or information storage and retrieval without permission in writing from the author.

This is a work of fiction. Names, characters, places, brands, media, and incidents are either the product of the author's imagination or are used fictitiously. The author acknowledges the trademarked status and trademark owners of various products referenced in this work of fiction, which have been used without permission. The publication/use of these trademarks is not authorized, associated with, or sponsored by the trademark owners.

Edited by Chereese Graves

www.nicsaint.com

Give feedback on the book at: info@nicsaint.com

facebook.com/nicsaintauthor
@nicsaintauthor

First Edition

Printed in the U.S.A

PURRFECT IMPASSE

Dead End Street

When Odelia and Chase are called to the scene of an apparent murder-suicide, the conclusion seems pretty straightforward. The Römers were facing serious financial difficulties brought on by their son's illness. But when a second and a third tragedy take place at walking distance from the cul-de-sac where the Römers lived, things suddenly aren't as obvious as they first appeared. And as the investigation progresses, the fractious relationship between the neighbors quickly becomes the focus. A lot of bad blood existed in what at first looked like the perfect suburb. So who killed the Römers? Find out in *Purrfect Impasse*, the latest installment in this blorange feline sleuth's chronicles.

PROLOGUE

*P*aul Römer had no idea what to expect when he walked into the Seven-Eleven. He had a big gun in his right hand and a bouquet of flowers in his left, and when he stepped up to the counter and saw the pimple-faced teenager's face turn white, a surge of embarrassment assailed him. He was definitely not cut out for this. But since he didn't have another choice... "Hands in the air!" he shouted, since the YouTube video explaining how to rob a convenience store had outlined that this was the magic formula for getting what you wanted under these circumstances. "And give me all the money in the cash register," he added on a side note. He thought for a moment about his next course of action but nothing came to mind. He'd watched that video about a dozen times, and still couldn't recall the particulars of the next part of the transaction.

Apparently, the pimple-faced kid knew, though, for with shaking hands he had emptied out the cash register and handed all of its contents to him. Now, that was quick service, the kind of service he liked to see. And so, as he tucked the money into the plastic bag he'd brought along for this purpose, he handed the flowers to the kid. He had hoped the person behind the checkout counter would be a pretty girl. In which case the flowers would have been justified as a way to diminish the ordeal he was forcing her to go through. But seeing as it was a kid, and considering he'd paid good money for those flowers, he didn't want them to go to waste, so he gave them to him anyway.

"Maybe you can give them to your girlfriend," he suggested. But when he took a closer look at the kid's braces and coke-bottle glasses, he amended that statement. "Or maybe to your mom."

The kid nodded quickly, took the flowers, then dropped them again, then said in a shaky voice, "Do you want fries with that, sir?"

"No, I don't want fries with that," he said. "Though I appreciate the gesture, kid."

And since he figured he'd done what he had come there to do, and couldn't think of anything else to say, he walked back out of the store. And he hadn't had to fire his gun even once.

He disappeared into the night, knowing full well that regular folk probably don't make their living robbing convenience stores. But also knowing that this was probably the only way he could safely and quickly supplement his income. And since he had plenty of other problems to concern himself with, he forgot about the plight the checkout clerk faced in having to explain to his boss that he'd just lost all of that day's earnings and focused on his own plight instead.

After all, if you have a sick kid at home in urgent need of a very expensive and almost unaffordable medical treatment in some distant country, a lot of your qualms go out of the window, and what you're left with is a simple but radical solution to a vexing problem.

He got into his car and sat for a moment, collecting his

thoughts. Then he took the money from the bag and began to place the bills on the car passenger seat, putting the twenties on the twenties and the fifties on the fifties and so on and so forth. Finally, he counted his little haul and figured that it was not a bad way to spend a pleasant evening. If he robbed another dozen or so of these convenience stores, and maybe a couple of gas stations, he might be able to get enough money together to pay for Hector's treatment.

He sighed deeply, shoved his key into the ignition and started the car. A dozen stores in a single night. It was possible, of course, logistically speaking, but not easy. But since he was all out of options, he figured that instead of worrying about the practical side of the endeavor, he should probably get on with it. And so he took off, aiming to head for the next store, and he would have arrived there in due course if he hadn't crossed the path of a deer who happened to pick that exact moment to cross the road. Instead of quickening its pace to get out of the path of the oncoming car, it just stood there, staring at him. Lucky for the deer, Paul was fully awake, adrenaline coursing through his veins from the holdup he'd just perpetrated, and so he managed to avoid hitting the deer and brought the car to a full stop. As he patted himself to ascertain he had broken no bones, he wondered if this was a sign that maybe the path he had chosen wasn't the right one after all.

CHAPTER 1

*D*ooley had been staring at me for the better part of the past five minutes, and frankly I was starting to feel my eyelids getting heavy and drooping closed. The urge to blink was so overpowering that finally I simply couldn't take it anymore, and so I blinked.

"I won!" Dooley cried jubilantly. "I won, Max, I won!"

"I know you won," I grumbled. It was a silly game that had been introduced into our household by none other than Harriet, who had engaged in this same pastime with Shanille, of all cats. For some reason it was all the rage, even though I didn't see what was so enjoyable about staring at someone and trying not to blink. Frankly speaking, to me, it was more like a child's game. Something Grace would probably enjoy once she was a little older and had a few friends.

"Let's do it again!" Dooley said. "Only this time let's make it more difficult."

"I think it's difficult enough as it is," I told him.

"Let's also tap each other's paws now. So every time you blink, I'll tap your paws, and then when I blink, you can tap mine."

I found the game a little tedious, to be honest, but since Dooley seemed to derive a lot of enjoyment from it, I decided to give him the satisfaction. And so I suppressed a groan, and the whole thing recommenced with the two of us staring at each other like absolute idiots and adding the tapping business to the rest of it. I didn't mind the blinking part so much, but every time Dooley tapped my paws, he accidentally forgot to retract his claws, which was a little annoying. And so finally I gave up, figuring I could probably find a better use of my time. "Okay, you win," I told him.

"I won!" he cried, pumping the air with his paws. "I won again! Three out of three!"

"Congratulations, buddy," I grunted. "Now can I finally take that nap?" With all this having to force myself to keep my eyes open, the thing I desired the most was to simply close my eyes now and not open them again for a very long time. Honestly a couple of hours of uninterrupted slumber sounded pretty good to me right now.

"Yeah, let's take a nap now," said Dooley as he yawned. "This game is a lot of fun, but it does make you tired, doesn't it, Max?"

"It certainly does," I agreed, and to show him how it was done, I put my head on my front paws and promptly dozed off. Or at least I would have dozed off if the living room door hadn't opened, and Odelia and Chase walked in, back from a night out on the town. They divested themselves of their coats, and out of sheer habit Odelia glanced at our bowls, making sure they were still full, our water bowls included, then joined us on the couch in the salon. While Chase turned on the television, we snuggled up to our human, and as silly as this may sound, suddenly I felt as if I'd arrived in heaven and that everything was all right with the world.

A strong scent filled my nostrils, and when I glanced up I saw that Chase had poured himself and Odelia a glass of wine, and they were sipping it and watching something on television that didn't hold a lot of interest to me. I closed my eyes again and was about to return to the Land of Nod when Gran walked in through the kitchen door, carrying Grace, who was clearly asleep.

"So how was your night out?" asked Gran.

"Oh, it was fine," said Odelia. "We had dinner and saw a movie."

"A date, huh?" said Gran with a wink. "That's the ticket. Gotta keep that love life exciting. When your granddad was still alive, and we were still together, he asked me out at least once a month. To keep things fresh, you know. I remember one night he took me to this restaurant with no lights on so we had to dine in the dark. It was a little weird but also really special. When you don't have your sense of sight, all the other senses are enhanced, you know, so the food tasted so much better, and then afterward we decided to continue the experiment by not turning on the light in the bedroom when we got home." She grinned. "The things we did—"

"All right, Gran," said Odelia with a laugh. "I don't think we need to hear all of that."

"You could learn a thing or two," said Gran. "You young people like to think you know it all. But you know nothing. There's a whole world out there of sensory excitement that you're only starting to explore."

"We'll explore it in our own time," Odelia assured her grandmother. "But right now, all I want to do," she added as she stifled a yawn, "is to go to bed and have a good night's sleep."

Gran tsk-tsked lightly. "Beds aren't meant to be slept in, you know. At least not only to be slept in. You should spice up your love life, you two. And I've got just the ticket."

"Gran, not now, please," said Odelia as she held up a hand.

"Oh, all right. But I've got a nice book that's going to

revolutionize the way you and Chase engage with each other. I'll see if I can't dig it out. It's got plenty of good stuff, and the woman who wrote it worked it all out herself, by experimenting with the different men in her life."

"She had different men, huh?"

"Absolutely. To keep things fresh, you gotta experiment." She eyed Grace for a moment. "Okay, so maybe not you guys, since you've got a kid. But us older folk, who don't have the care of a kid anymore—experimentation is key to staying healthy and happy!"

"Good for you," Chase said as he turned off the television. He stretched. "Let's hit the hay, babe. I have to get up early tomorrow."

"Yeah, me too," said Odelia.

And so they more or less ushered Gran out of their home, put Grace to bed, and took care of those pre-bedtime arrangements humans like to engage in, such as brushing their teeth, removing whatever makeup they have smeared on their faces, putting on their pajamas, and generally spending way more time than I would before actually retiring for the night. And then when they were finally in bed, they didn't go to sleep immediately. First, they had to talk a little. And then they had to read a book and give their phones a final once-over. It all seemed a little self-defeating to me, since us cats simply sleep where we lay, and we don't even brush our teeth, put on pajamas, or generally waste any time before doing what we do best, which is napping. But then we all know that humans have strange habits that are hard to explain sometimes.

At long last, they turned out the light, and just when I was finally about to relax, Chase's phone chimed out a penetrating tune. With a groan, he picked the offending object from the nightstand, and as Odelia turned on the light again, he said, "It's your uncle." He put the phone to his ear and listened for a moment. His face sagged. "I'll be there in ten, Chief."

"What happened?" asked Odelia as she rubbed her eyes.

"There's been a murder," Chase announced as he swung his feet from underneath the comforter again. "An entire family has been killed in what looks like a murder-suicide."

"Oh, God," said Odelia, as she also removed the comforter.

"You don't have to come," he said.

"Of course I do," she said, ending that particular argument. Then she turned to me and Dooley, who had been reposing at the foot of the bed. "And you guys are also coming," she said in a voice that brooked no contest.

Moments later, she was dropping Grace off at her parents' house, causing Gran to comment that this was not the kind of love-life-enhancing type of fun she had in mind for them, but accepting her role as a babysitter without reservations, and then we were on our way to the scene of the tragedy.

Somehow, I had the impression that it was going to be a little while before I was going to get to take that nap.

CHAPTER 2

It didn't take us long to get where we needed to be, which was a very nice villa on the outskirts of town. It was a nice neighborhood, with similar houses all located in a cul-de-sac. Not the kind of neighborhood where you expect some major massacre to take place. Then again, tragedies can occur anywhere, in any family, and apparently now it had happened there.

We got out of Chase's squad car and walked up the drive, which was teeming with police and emergency vehicles. I wondered if we'd be forced to enter the premises because, to be honest, I'm a little squeamish about blood and awful scenes. I know it may come as something of a surprise, considering I'm a feline detective, but that's the way I roll. I see myself more as one of those armchair detectives, you know, like that fella who used to sit in his chair sniffing flowers all day, and his assistant brought him his cases on a platter and did all the legwork for him. Of course, since I'm not famous enough or rich enough to be able to afford an assistant willing to do my legwork, I have to venture out and do all of that myself. I could always employ Dooley, of course, but I very much doubt he'd be willing to go out there on his own and gather clues, sniff at discarded cigarette butts, and generally act as my Dr. Watson/Captain Hastings/Archie Goodwin. After all, it's not as if I have the funds to pay him for his efforts. Also, I'm not sure he wouldn't trample all over the evidence and spoil things for the other detectives at the scene.

One of those detectives now approached us and shook his head. "It's pretty darn heartbreaking," he warned us. "If you don't have to go in there, you better don't."

He addressed himself to Odelia as he said this, leading the latter to give him a sort of icy look.

"I'm fine," she assured him.

For some reason, male detectives still seem to think that the female of the species is too squeamish to deal with the harsher aspects of tackling crime and solving murders. Then again, maybe some females are squeamish that way. I know for a fact that Harriet, our good friend, hates to enter these dreadful scenes of murder and mayhem, though that could also have something to do with the fact that she hates getting blood all over her precious paws.

We entered the house through the kitchen and soon found ourselves in the living room, where apparently the big tragedy had taken place. I will spare you the gruesome details, but suffice it to say that no less than three people lost their lives that night. According to the police officers present at the scene, these were Paul Römer, his wife Maria Römer, and their young son Hector Römer, who was only six years old. All of them had died from gunshot wounds to the chest, apart from Mr. Römer himself, who had died from a gunshot wound to the right temple. He was also the one suspected of having caused the death of his wife and son before turning his gun on himself and ending his own life.

"Terrible tragedy," said Odelia's uncle, who was also

present. "I knew her personally, you know, Maria. She used to work at the station for a while as a typist, but when her son was born, she decided to stay home."

Maria Römer herself was on the couch, along with her son, and had apparently been watching television when the husband had gone berserk and started inflicting grievous bodily harm on his family. The man himself was lying in front of the television, where he had fallen.

I didn't need to sniff around for clues to know that the scene was pretty clear-cut, so Dooley and I walked out of there as quickly as we could.

We found ourselves in the kitchen, where an enterprising police officer had put on a pot of coffee, and several of Uncle Alec's officers were enjoying a cup of the bracing brew after the ordeal they'd gone through having to witness what one person can do to his family. They all seemed pretty gutted, I have to say, and I could understand why. After all, they were all parents themselves and probably couldn't imagine something like this happening to their families.

Uncle Alec joined us in the kitchen, and so did Odelia, while Chase decided to stay behind and take a closer look at the victims and the evidence. Crime scene people were going over the crime scene with a fine-tooth comb, and so it was probably best if they weren't disturbed in this vital part of the job of determining what exactly had happened and who was responsible for what.

"Did you know the husband?" asked Odelia.

"Not really, no," said Uncle Alec as he stripped out of the protective suit he'd been wearing to make sure he didn't contaminate the crime scene, as the jargon goes. Odelia and Chase were wearing similar outfits, and Dooley and I should probably have worn the same type of gear. But since we are cats we tend to slip in and out of places without people paying us too much attention.

"So what do you think happened?" asked Odelia.

Uncle Alec shrugged. "Looks pretty straightforward to me. Obviously, the guy lost it and killed his wife and kid and then turned the gun on himself. Though why he would have done such a terrible thing beats me. I hadn't been in touch with Maria in a couple of years, so I can't tell you if they were having financial problems or other issues." He frowned. "I do know that Maria was very close to Dolores when she worked at the station. Those two always took their lunch breaks together, and as far as I remember also saw each other socially, outside of office hours. So maybe you should go talk to her. But break the news gently, will you? Dolores may look like a tough cookie, but she was very fond of Maria, and she'll probably be pretty devastated about what happened."

"So what happened, Max?" asked Dooley as we walked out of the kitchen to leave the humans to determine what their next course of action was going to be. "Why did that man murder his wife and his son?"

"We don't know yet, Dooley," I said. "Maybe they had financial problems, like Uncle Alec suggested, and he just couldn't cope anymore. Or maybe they got into a fight, and he lost his mind. We just don't know."

What I did know was that we should probably put our best paw forward and talk to any pets we could find. As far as I had been able to ascertain, the Römers didn't have pets themselves, or else we would have noticed. Which was a shame on the one hand since we wouldn't be able to ask them what happened, but on the other hand, it was also a blessing since they wouldn't suddenly have become bereft of their beloved humans and have to lose their home, which is never a fun prospect.

But since the cul-de-sac consisted of at least eight houses, I figured we had a pretty good chance of finding at least a couple of pets there we could talk to and maybe get a clearer picture of what had happened that night. Pets are notoriously curious and aren't shy about it either. So chances were that someone had seen or heard something. So while Uncle Alec's officers went door-to-door to talk to the neighbors, Dooley and I did the same thing but by entering backyards in search of feline or canine witnesses to the tragedy.

It didn't take us long to hit upon our first possible witness in the form of... a turtle. The turtle belonged to the direct next-door neighbor of the Römers, and we found her lounging in the backyard, munching on a blade of grass, as turtles are wont to do. Beyond her, I could see some nice flower beds, though for some odd reason next to every flower someone had planted a plastic fork, with the tines pointing up.

"Hi there," I said by way of greeting.

The turtle lifted its wrinkly head to give us a look of appreciation. "Two nice young cats paying me a visit," she said in a sort of croaky voice. "Now isn't this cozy?"

"It's not exactly a social call," I hastened to point out. "We work for the police department, you see, and we're interviewing potential witnesses to a crime that took place next door."

"What crime?" asked the turtle as she stopped chewing the grass and gave us a look of alarm. "Did someone... steal my turtle tank? Or did they steal my food?"

"Nobody stole your tank," I assured the turtle. "Or your food. But a crime was committed next door, and three people died, so we were wondering if by chance you happened to overhear something or saw something in the past couple of hours? The sounds of an argument, perhaps, or shots being fired?"

"Oh no! Did they shoot at my turtle tank? Did they shoot up my food?"

"Nobody shot at your turtle tank," I said, starting to think this turtle had a particularly one-track mind. "And nobody shot up your food. Three people died, your neighbors the Römers? And so we were wondering if you could tell us what happened since they lived right next door."

In fact, from where we were standing, we could look straight into the Römers' backyard, so if the turtle had been where she was now, she should have heard those gunshots and maybe had heard an argument taking place.

But the turtle shook her head. "I'm not sure what you're asking me," she said. "I didn't hear anything, and I also didn't see anything."

"So, no sound of shots being fired?" I asked for good measure.

She shook her head again. "I did hear a woman scream, if that's helpful."

"What woman? Was it Maria Römer?"

"I'm not sure," said the old turtle with a pensive look as she thought hard and tried to throw her mind back.

"By the way, what's your name?" asked Dooley, who is a lot politer than I am, I have to say, since I had forgotten this first rule of polite conversation in my haste to get tangible results first. "My name is Dooley," he added, "and this is my friend Max."

The turtle smiled, showing us that she appreciated a certain sense of decorum. "Hi, Dooley. Hi, Max. Two strapping young cats like you paying me a visit. My, my, isn't this a nice surprise? So while you're here, could you perhaps give me a helping paw?"

"Oh, absolutely," said Dooley, even though we probably had other fish to fry than to give lone turtles helping paws. But then I guess Dooley is more about letting his heart speak and not his mind, which makes him a better cat than me since I have a habit of focusing on the end result and tend to forget such social niceties as helping out a turtle. "What can we do for you, Miss…"

"Rita," said the turtle. "And it's Mrs. My husband's name is Ralph. He's in the tank right now dozing. Which is why I was so upset when you told me about those shots being fired since if those crooks took a potshot at the tank, they might have hit him, you see."

"But why would crooks take potshots at your tank?" asked Dooley.

"Well, there's this gang of kids, see, who like to break into houses and steal stuff? And they also like to shoot stuff up and generally make a nuisance of themselves. It's been a real scourge on this neighborhood, which used to be such a nice one, once upon a time."

"A gang of kids has been terrorizing the neighborhood?" I asked.

"Oh, absolutely. It's been going on for months now, and in spite of the police patrolling the street and trying to get rid of these kids, nothing seems to help. They were here this afternoon, setting off firecrackers and racing up and down the street on their motorcycles and generally making a big fuss. The police finally arrived, and they chased them away, but I'm sure they'll be back tomorrow, and everything will just start all over again. It's an absolute disgrace."

"Yeah, I can imagine it must be extremely annoying having to live under these circumstances," I agreed. I pointed to the plastic forks. "What are those for?"

"Mh?" She glanced over, and gave us a little grin. "Those are actually against you guys."

"Against us?" asked Dooley, much surprised.

"Yeah, Mike—that's our human—doesn't like cats, and he planted those to keep you out. And dogs, of course."

It was true that those forks didn't exactly look appealing. I wouldn't like to put down my paw on one of those. They may have been made of plastic and thus slightly yielding to pressure, but the experience probably would not be a pleasant one.

The turtle had finally arrived at the backdoor, which was locked but also had one of those pet flaps that are all the rage, and of which Odelia and Chase also have one to allow us to come and go as we please. The turtle moved inside, and Dooley and I had no other recourse but to follow her in.

"I wonder what she wants us to do?" I whispered.

"Oh, probably to pick up a piece of lettuce that fell from their tank," said Dooley. "She's such a nice old turtle, isn't she, Max?"

"She is," I agreed, though I sincerely wondered if we shouldn't be interviewing other potential witnesses. Though this story about the scream she'd heard fascinated me, and I wondered if that could have been Maria Römer she had overheard before her husband went berserk.

Rita had walked up to the turtle tank she had been referring to, and she was visibly relieved when she saw it hadn't been shot up, and that her husband Ralph was still resting peacefully inside the enclosure. A sort of ramp led up to the tank, which had been placed on a table in front of the kitchen window.

"My husband is not well," she revealed. "Not that he's sick or anything, since the vet has given him a clean bill of health after our last checkup, but he tires easily and sleeps a lot these days. He's older than me, you know, and I know what they say about dating an older turtle: that one day you'll lose him while you're still in your prime. But I didn't care, and I still don't. He was such a handsome dashing hunk when we were younger, you know, and I still find him very attractive."

She gazed lovingly up at her husband, though when I studied the sleeping turtle I failed to see the appeal. Then again, I'm not a turtle myself, of course, so that's probably why I didn't find Ralph particularly hunkish.

"Ralph!" she suddenly yelled. "Ralph, we got visitors!"

Ralph opened one eye and studied us lazily. I had the impression of the eye of Godzilla opening and taking in a pair of unwanted trespassers before rearing up and devouring them whole.

"Cats!" he growled, and didn't sound all that happy to see us. "Why did you bring a pair of cats into our home, Rita!"

"They're not cats, they're police detectives," Rita explained. "Something happened next door and they want to know if we saw something."

"What happened? What are you talking about?" asked Ralph as he opened his second eye and now was staring at me with a penetrating gaze that I found particularly unnerving.

"Oh, I don't know. At first, I thought they'd shot up our tank, but apparently something else happened. Probably those annoying kids again."

"Your neighbors were murdered," I said, deciding that maybe this turtle was a better witness than his wife. "The Römers? All three of them died tonight, and so we're trying to figure out what happened."

At that moment, the doorbell sounded, and we could hear a noise upstairs that told us that Rita and Ralph's owners had heard the bell and were ready to come down the stairs to open the door.

"Now what?" said Ralph.

"That's probably our colleagues from the police department," I said, "eager to have a chat with your humans and ask them if they can shed some light on the terrible events next door."

"They won't know what happened, since they weren't home," said Ralph. "They were out all evening."

"They like to go out on a Friday night," Rita explained. "Mostly sports games, since they're nuts about sports. Though sometimes they'll go out to dinner. They like to keep the love light burning, you see." She giggled.

"Same thing with our humans," Dooley said. "They also like to keep the love light burning, or at least that's what Odelia's grandmother advises, though I'm not sure I understand what she means by that."

"Well, it means that you have to keep that passion going," Rita explained, even though I really did not want to know about the passion her humans shared. "At first, when kids get together, they're all frisky and can't keep their hands off each other, see? But then once they've been together for a while, they stop being all over each other and get staid and settled in their ways. But you have to combat that and make sure that you're still all over each other. Which means you have to touch each other, and caress each other, and kiss and generally show your partner how much you care." She had approached her husband and was now demonstrating exactly what she meant by touching his shell and giving him gentle nudges, to which he didn't seem to respond in any way that I could discern. At most, he seemed annoyed by these overt attempts at friskiness.

"Oh, you mean like Harriet and Brutus," said Dooley, nodding. "They're our good friends and housemates, you see, and they're always spending time in the rose bushes, and once I caught them and they were hugging and kissing. Though when I arrived, they suddenly stopped and told me to go away, so I didn't think they liked that I saw what they were doing."

Rita giggled again. "I don't mind if people see what me and Ralph are up to. I like to rub his shell like this," she said and did as she indicated. "And I like to give him little kisses on the top of his head, which he loves." She carried out this threat by showering Ralph's head with tiny kisses, to which Ralph responded by giving her the evil eye. Clearly, he wasn't as fond of these little signs of affection as his partner seemed to think.

"Okay, so what do you want us to help you with?" I asked, feeling as if we were simply wasting our time. Also, I'm not really all that interested in the love life of pet turtles.

"Could you please help me shift the tank?" asked Rita. "It's too close to the window, you see, and when the sun shines in, it gets entirely too hot in there. But of course our humans have no idea, and since we can't tell them, we have to escape from the tank in the daytime, since it's almost like a sauna in there."

"Absolutely," said Dooley. Since apparently we didn't have anything else to do than to help a turtle couple shift their tank, we put our backs into it and shoved the table on which the tank was standing further away from the window. This accomplished, I could hear distinct voices from the corridor, indicating that Ralph and Rita's owners were now busily chatting with the police. But since we had to move a turtle tank, I couldn't hear what they were saying. I guess a cat detective has these little moments of frustration. I bore up as well as I could, still holding out a faint but dwindling hope that we would glean some information from this old but still frisky couple.

"Okay, so about that scream," I reminded Rita. "Who did the screaming, and what do you think caused her to scream?"

Rita thought for a moment. "Maria," she said. "At first, I thought it was our own human, since she has a tendency to scream when she gets upset."

"And she gets upset a lot," Ralph commented.

"But then I figured that since it was coming from next door, and also our humans had left home to go to the ball game, it couldn't be Mikaela, so it had to be Maria."

"Who never screams," Ralph pointed out.

"No, but she did this time."

"What time was this?" I asked. Now we were finally getting somewhere.

"Um… seven-thirty maybe? Or eight? I know this because our humans had left around seven, so they would be on time for the game. They hate to be late, especially Mike, who's a stickler for punctuality. And a little time had passed since they'd left, maybe like half an hour or so. I was in the backyard at the time, and the scream did seem to come from the Römers. I remember wondering if maybe she had cut herself, you know. When our human cut herself once on a very sharp knife, she screamed so loud the Römers actually came running, since they figured someone must have broken in and threatened Mikaela at knifepoint or something."

"But it wasn't Mikaela," I said, hoping to make her move along a little quicker.

"No, it wasn't Mikaela, since she and Mike had left by that time. To the ball game."

"Okay, so what else happened?" I asked.

She glanced at Ralph, who was eyeing us intently. "Nothing," she said simply. "Someone screamed, I thought it was probably Maria, and that's it. Nothing else happened."

"So… no sound of shots being fired?"

"No, nothing like that," said Rita.

Which was a little odd, I thought. When a shot is fired, it makes a lot of noise, and since we were right next door, Rita should have heard those shots.

"I have to add I'm a little hard of hearing," she admitted. "And also, I've been inside most of the evening, so if these so-called shots you keep referring to were indeed fired, I wouldn't have heard them."

"What about you, sir?" I asked, turning to Ralph.

"What about me?" Ralph grumbled, still continuing to be both unhelpful and unfriendly.

"Did you hear any gunshots? Or that scream your wife is referring to?"

"I heard nothing," said Ralph.

"Like I told you, Ralph sleeps a lot," said Rita. "Not that he's sick or anything, but just that he's tired a lot lately. Isn't that right, honey bunch?"

"None of their business," Ralph grumbled.

He was probably right. It wasn't any of our business that he wasn't the handsome hunk he used to be, making the hearts of female turtles beat faster. But still, he could have given us something.

"How was the relationship between the Römers?" I asked. "Did they get along well? Or did they fight a lot?"

"Oh, they were a lovely couple," said Rita. "Very loving and very attached to each other. And of course, they loved their little boy to death." She sucked in a breath. "I probably shouldn't have said that."

"No, it's fine," I encouraged her. "So they loved each other, and they loved their boy. So no arguments that you heard? No fights?"

She shook her head. "Never. They were as devoted a couple as I've ever seen, and trust me, I've seen many couples. Mike and Mikaela have a wide circle of friends, and a lot of those couples are not exactly role models, let me tell you. There's this one couple they know, and they just can't stop arguing from the moment they walk in till the moment they leave. It's absolutely dreadful."

"None of our business," Ralph grumbled.

"But it is our business, honey bunch," said Rita. "They're our friends."

"They're not our friends," he pointed out. "They're our human's friends, so it's none of our business." He gestured to me and Dooley with his wrinkly turtle head. "And it's definitely none of *their* business."

In the meantime, the police officers seemed to have concluded their business, since the door closed, and we could hear footsteps on the stairs again. And since I had the impression that we'd gotten as much out of Rita and Ralph as we ever would, I decided to adopt an unorthodox approach and stick my nose where it probably didn't belong. I turned to Dooley, gave him a subtle sign, and together we left the kitchen and headed into the corridor.

Ralph shouted after us, "Hey, where are you going? Come back here! It's none of your business!"

"Oh, Ralph, don't shout," said Rita. "You know what the doctor said. It's bad for your blood pressure."

"Tell those cats to come back here!" said Ralph.

"I will do nothing of the kind. They helped us move our tank, and so I'm not going to tell them anything. In fact, you should thank them."

"Oh, nuts," the formerly handsome hunk and ladies' turtle grumbled.

CHAPTER 3

Dooley and I tiptoed up the stairs, knowing full well that the turtles wouldn't be able to give us away. Before long, we were seated at the bedroom door and listened in as Ralph and Rita's humans discussed recent events.

"I still can't believe it," said Mike. "For Paul to shoot his wife and kid and then to kill himself? That doesn't sound like the Paul we know."

"I knew this was going to happen," said his wife Mikaela. "Haven't I told you that Paul is one of those dangerous types? Like a volcano, you just know that one day they're going to erupt, and that once they do, it's going to be really ugly."

"No, you never told me that," said her husband.

"I did! Last summer at the neighborhood picnic, I overheard the two of them arguing over by the table with the cupcakes Raquel had baked for the occasion, and I could tell that Paul had a lot of repressed anger. That man was a psychopath in the making, honey."

"But why kill the kid? That poor little fella hadn't done anything wrong, and now he's dead. Okay, so I know they were in trouble, but why take it out on his kid? That's what I don't understand."

"He must have gone mad, that's the only thing I can think of. Just lost it and went completely crazy."

For a moment, silence reigned, and then he said, "Now I can't sleep."

"Me neither. I keep thinking about that poor woman. Her final moments, she must have seen it coming, and she probably wanted to protect her boy, but there was nothing she could do." She sighed deeply. "It's at moments like this that I'm actually glad that we didn't bring any kids into this world, Mike. It's not a world fit for those poor innocent babies. In fact, it's probably considered a crime these days to have a kid since you just know they're going to be faced with this kind of ugliness all around."

"Yeah, I guess you're right," said her husband.

"Speaking about ugliness, we probably should have told that cop that those hooligans have been up to their old tricks again."

"What do you mean?"

"I couldn't sleep, so I went downstairs to drink some water, and I saw how the backdoor was unlocked again. I locked it before we went to bed, I'm sure I did, but I saw that it wasn't locked anymore. So they must have broken in again, probably looking for money or whatever."

"Those kids," her husband grumbled.

"And the lock wasn't tampered with either. But the door was open, and I'm one hundred percent sure I locked it before we went to bed."

"Maybe they managed to use the pet flap to get in," Mike suggested.

"Possibly," his wife allowed. "Although to reach the lock from the pet flap is not so easy, unless they've got really long arms. No, they must have found some other way to open the door."

"Was anything missing?"

"I haven't really looked, but I don't think so. It's almost as if they came in, looked around, figured there wasn't anything worth taking, and left again the same way they came in."

"At least they didn't harm the turtles," said Mike.

"Don't say that, Mike," she said, sounding pained. "I wouldn't forgive myself if those kids harmed Ralph or Rita."

"They won't harm the turtles. Though, of course, they could if they're high on drugs. There's no telling what they might do if that happens."

"I think we should move, Mike. Didn't I tell you about a million times that we should move? First those hooligans terrorizing the streets, and now Paul and Maria. This neighborhood is going to the dogs, and if we stay here one minute longer, our house will lose its value, and we won't even be able to sell it anymore."

"We are going to move, honey. And that's a promise," said her husband.

I felt as if we'd heard enough, and even though I had hoped to glean some vital piece of information, clearly these two had no idea what happened next door either. And so we snuck back down the stairs and were just about to head through the pet flap and out into the backyard when Rita said something that made us pause in our tracks.

"I've just remembered, you guys," she said. "After that scream I heard? I think I heard someone say 'Please don't leave me.' I've just been thinking and thinking, and I'm pretty sure that's what happened. I wasn't sure before, which is why I didn't say anything, but now that I've given it some more thought…" She nodded fervently. "'Please don't leave me.' Sounds pretty ominous considering what happened next, don't you think?"

"So who said it?" I asked. "Was it a male voice or a female voice?"

"Definitely a male voice," said Rita, nodding.

"And was it Paul Römer who said it, you think?"

She thought for a moment, even going so far as to close her eyes as she threw her mind back. "I'm not sure," she said finally. "It could have been Paul, of course, but I wasn't paying a lot of attention at the time since I was so busy looking for that worm."

"What worm?" asked Dooley, interested. As a fan of the Discovery Channel, he takes a keen interest in everything that has to do with both plant life and animal life.

"Well, it's been raining a lot these past couple of days," said Rita, happy for this chance to elucidate on a topic that clearly interested her a great deal. "And so the earth has been teeming with worms, which as you can probably imagine made me and Ralph very happy. But there was this one worm that kept eluding me. A big fat specimen that Ralph said he had his eye on. And so I've been trying to catch it for the better part of the past three days, and finally I thought I saw it this evening, lounging underneath a leaf, but when I got there, it had just escaped by digging into the ground. I tried to grab it by the tail, but it was too fast for me. I even tried going after it, but I couldn't reach it, and the only thing I ended up with for my trouble was a snout full of sand, if you please!" She laughed at her own misfortune, even though I could tell that Ralph hadn't been happy that the worm he'd selected for dinner had managed to escape his wife's endeavors.

"You should have gone after it when I told you to," he grumbled. "Of course, by the time you finally got a move on, it was gone."

"Ralph loves a nice juicy worm from time to time," Rita revealed. "And when he doesn't get it, he gets cranky."

I had the impression that even when Ralph did get the worms he desired, he still was cranky. He was just that kind of turtle.

"Okay, so a woman screaming, possibly Maria Römer, and then a male voice that said, 'Please don't leave me,'" I reiterated. "So the scream came first? Or the voice?"

She frowned. "Um, I think first there was the scream, and then the voice." She nodded as if to convince herself. "Yeah, I'm pretty sure that's how it happened."

"So your humans were talking about a break-in?" I said. "Mikaela said she locked the back door when they came home after the ball game and before she and Mike went to bed, and then when she couldn't sleep and came down to drink some water, she discovered that the door was unlocked. So did you happen to notice any intruders breaking into the house?"

Rita and Ralph shared a look. "I didn't see anything," said Ralph.

"No, I didn't see anything either," said Rita. "Though I have to say, I'm a very sound sleeper. Once I fall asleep, you can fire off a cannon, and I won't wake up."

"Same here," said Ralph. He narrowed his eyes at me. "So what was with all the spying? Why did you have to sneak upstairs and spy on our humans?"

"Oh, just leave them be," said Rita. "Haven't I told you? They're police cats, and police cats are always snooping around and asking questions and generally digging into people's private lives trying to catch them about stuff."

"Apart from the door being unlocked," said Dooley, "Mike and Mikaela didn't have a lot of interesting information to share. Isn't that right, Max?"

"No, they didn't," I confirmed. "They were surprised by what happened with the Römers, though Mikaela said she'd been expecting something like this to happen. She described

Paul Römer as a volcano about to erupt. Though I had the impression that Mike didn't agree with her on that assessment."

"And also, they're thinking about moving away from the neighborhood," said Dooley helpfully. "But they're afraid they won't find a buyer for the house after what happened with the hooligan kids and also the murders next door."

Rita had pressed a paw to her chest. "Oh, my goodness. There's talk about moving again? But I like it here so much. It's just the ideal neighborhood for us, isn't it, Ralph?"

"I love it here," grumbled Ralph. "Apart from those nasty worms who keep wriggling away every time you try to catch them, we got a pretty good life here."

"It's paradise," Rita said. "Absolute paradise."

The couple seemed to have conveniently forgotten about the so-called hooligans and also about people murdering each other. Then again, to a turtle, a nice supply of worms is probably more important than any hooligans or any murders taking place. Life is all about priorities, after all, and for some of us a nice juicy worm is definitely priority number one.

As we finally left the house, I wondered how significant this scream Rita had heard, and the whispered words 'Please don't leave me' were to our investigation. But since they could have come from next door, I figured they must be important, and the first chance we got, we'd relay the information to Odelia. We didn't see her at the Römer place, so I figured we might as well pay a visit to the couple's other neighbors and investigate some more. I just hoped we'd find pets in a slightly better mood than Ralph, since the last thing I needed was another curmudgeon.

But when we arrived in the backyard of the next house, we quickly determined these people didn't own any pets of any description, so we skipped it and moved on. At the next house we found ourselves in luck since the backyard was occupied by a small yapper answering to the name Fifi. It was a dog of the Chihuahua type who was more than happy to lend us a helping paw.

"Oh, of course I knew the Römers," said Fifi, who was a smallish canine with a sort of fringe that hung in her eyes, causing her to blink a lot. Clearly, she was in urgent need of a haircut. And as she told us her story, she practically vibrated with excitement, as these little lapdogs often do. "Very nice couple. Very nice indeed. Every time my human was in urgent need of some advice on cooking, she would head over to the Römers and ask Maria Römer, who was always happy to help. And when she needed a handyman, she would consult with Paul Römer, who was very handy and prided himself on having done most of the work on the house himself."

"Were they a devoted couple, you would say?" I asked.

She didn't even have to think twice about that. "Oh, absolutely. Those two loved each other so much! Loved each other to bits. Even at the neighborhood picnic last summer, they were all over each other all the time. When the group brought out the folding chairs and sat in a circle, Maria sat on her husband's lap, and she was the only one of the wives present to do that. All the others were in separate chairs, and some of them even sat as far away from each other as humanly possible. But not Paul and Maria. Hugging, kissing, touching… They were clearly crazy about each other, and also about their little boy, whom they just loved ever so much."

"Did you ever notice them arguing?" I asked.

"Never," said Fifi. "Never once did I hear a bad word. They didn't even gossip about each other behind the other person's back, like many couples will do. No, they were a united and devoted couple, as much in love now as when they married."

"Okay, so did you happen to hear a scream at around seven-thirty or eight o'clock?" I asked.

Fifi thought for a moment. "No, I can't say I did. But I was probably inside at that time being fed. And when I'm eating, I kinda tune everything out, you know. My mealtimes are sacred, and I hate to be disturbed. Why? Was there a scream?"

"According to Rita, who lives next to the Römers, there was."

She laughed. "Oh, but you shouldn't put too much stock in what Rita has to say. She's always making stuff up. Only the other day she claimed to have caught ten big worms and fed them to Ralph. When I know for a fact that she didn't catch any. So whatever she says, you should probably take with a big pinch of salt."

"She also told us that she heard a man say the words, 'Please don't leave me,'" said Dooley.

"Again, don't believe a word that turtle says. She's the biggest source of gossip in this neighborhood, and one hundred percent of what she says is pure drivel. She told everyone who would listen last month that her humans had won the lottery, and that they were moving to Florida where they were going to live next door to Dwayne Johnson. But of course, nothing happened. And when I asked her about it last week, she said the money hadn't arrived in their bank account yet, as these things take time. But once those millions arrived they were definitely going to move away from here since she hated it here, and so did Ralph, and so did their humans."

It was certainly food for thought, as Rita had assured us that the last thing she wanted was to move. It made me wonder what else she had lied about. And since Fifi didn't have any other constructive information to share with us, we said our goodbyes and returned to the Römer place, deciding to see if Odelia and Chase had turned up already. As it turned out, they had, and so I decided to relay the information we had discovered, causing Odelia to give us a thoughtful look and jot down a couple of notes on her digital notepad.

"So what did you find out?" asked Dooley.

"Just that the Römers were in big financial trouble," said Odelia. "Their son was suffering from some kind of very rare type of kidney cancer, and his treatment was costing them a fortune, money that they didn't have. So that must have put a considerable strain on the family. But apart from that, everyone we talked to confirmed that they were a very loving couple, and very devoted to each other and to their little boy. They're all pretty shaken up by what happened."

We were in the backyard, where we could talk in private since most people don't think it's normal when a cat talks to their human, or the other way around. But then Odelia is one of those rare humans who *can* talk to us, which is very handy in cases like tonight's when a crime has been committed, and she sends us out into the field, so to speak, to interrogate other pets and put our ear to the ground. After we were done telling her what we had learned, she said that her uncle was convinced that what we saw was what happened: Paul Römer had lost his mind and had killed his wife and son before killing himself with the same gun. And if what she had learned about the boy's disease and the couple's financial problems was true, that was probably the motive for Paul's dramatic decline into madness causing him to end the lives of three people.

And since it was late already, she and Chase decided that it was probably best to return home for now and have some sleep, and then start the investigation afresh in the morning since there wasn't a whole lot more we could find out tonight.

Half an hour later, we were home again, with me and Dooley asleep at the foot of the bed and our humans snoring away gently. Grace was in her cot, also asleep, and generally the world had turned quiet and peaceful once again. But try as I might, I still couldn't get the conflicting testimony of Fifi and Rita the turtle out of my mind. Was there a scream? And was there a male voice beseeching someone not to leave him? And did that have any bearing on the tragedy that had occurred that night? I hoped we'd find out more in the morning. Though if Uncle Alec had his way, this investigation would probably be closed with the conclusions he had outlined to his niece and to Chase. And somehow I wasn't convinced it was as straightforward as that.

CHAPTER 4

Jim Ward had been tending to his lovely little patch in his local community garden when a drop falling on the back of his neck told him that he better get a move on since the rain the weather forecast had been warning about had finally arrived. The big drop had been cold and made him shiver, so he drew his cap deeper over his eyes, shrugged into his raincoat, and straightened up. He surveyed his little spot of delight with a deep-seated sense of pride. Due to circumstances out of his control, he couldn't tend to his own garden, so he counted himself lucky to be one of the few who had been granted permission to develop this small part of the bigger community gardens that had been made available by Hampton Cove's town council. His main interest was flowers, though some of his fellow gardeners liked to plant tomatoes or other vegetables and also herbs and such.

He glanced over to the little patch next to his own, and wondered where his neighbor could possibly be. Bill Taylor was just as avid a gardener as he was, and usually he was out here before dawn to tend to his own lovely little plot. Being retired and in the possession of a wealth of time, Bill spent most days at the community gardens, up before dawn and often home after dark. Jim and Bill had developed a firm friendship over the years and gave each other tips and pointers and generally enjoyed each other's company. So for Bill not to show up that morning was surprising, to say the least. Then again, maybe he had somewhere he needed to be. As far as Jim knew his friend originally hailed from Boston, and he still had relatives up there, though they rarely saw each other. He was a private man, Bill was, and even though the two friends had known each other for years, Jim still didn't know a whole lot about the guy. Just that he'd been a businessman before he took early retirement, and that he didn't have either wife or kids, just like Jim himself.

He wondered if he should drop by Bill's apartment to see if everything was all right. At their age something could always happen. Then again, it was probably nothing. And besides, with the heavy rains being forecast, Bill had probably decided to stay home today and sit out the storm.

He glanced over to another plot of land that was the bane of both his and Bill's existence. It belonged to a man named Oliver McDonald, and contrary to the unwritten rule about keeping your personal plot neat and tidy, this one was overgrown with weeds and looked absolutely terrible. Clearly Oliver simply didn't care about maintaining his part of the gardens. Jim and Bill had even considered complaining to the town council about it, but for some reason that didn't feel right to them. They weren't the type of people who were in the habit of lodging complaints about their fellow man, even if that fellow man was allowing his weeds to run amok.

The rain was really coming down hard now, and he hurried to the garden house that sat at the edge of his patch and hurried inside to be out of the rain. He didn't mind the weather. In fact, it was a good thing that it was raining, and as he watched his young plants being gently pummeled by those fats drops of rain, he thought it was exactly what they needed and that it would make them grow that much quicker.

And as he stood there, hidden from view, suddenly he thought he caught something from the corner of his eye. It was a dark shadow moving beyond his field of vision. As he looked over, he saw that a figure dressed in a green hoodie was traversing the different gardens. He didn't think he recognized the figure, though since the person was entirely hidden from view inside that hoodie, it was hard to know for sure.

The person moved out of sight and was soon gone, swallowed up by the darkness that had descended upon the world. Rivulets of rain poured off the corrugated roof of his shed, and as the rain pounded a musical rhythm above his head, he soon forgot all about the mysterious stranger.

* * *

RAIN WAS COMING DOWN HARD as Farmer Giles herded his cows into the barn. The weather had suddenly turned inclement, and even though his herd of cows was used to a little bad weather, they were already soaked to the skin, so he felt it was probably more judicious to put them inside where they would be dry. His vet had warned him that some of his cows who were pregnant might be adversely affected if they were outside for too long in bad weather conditions and that he should take extra special care to make sure they were well taken care of at all times. And since he essentially was fond of his animals, he felt he should probably do as Vena Aleman had suggested and make sure his cows were safe and dry in their barn. And anyway, it was coming up on their milking time, so he might as well push things up a little and get it over with.

And he was just ushering in the last of his herd when a man came hurrying up to him. It was Mark, the son of his neighbors Harry and Jessica Turner, and he was yelling something that Giles couldn't hear over the noise of the storm, which had really broken over the area by that point.

Once Mark had reached him and entered the barn, Giles saw that he was soaking wet and also out of breath. "It's Mom and Dad!" Mark said once he'd caught his breath. "They're..." He swallowed convulsively as he stared at the farmer with a sort of wild look in his eyes.

"Take deep breaths," Giles advised his neighbor's son. He knew that Mark was a good kid who helped out at the farm from time to time on weekends and holidays. He had recently turned fourteen and loved to help out around the farm, though strictly speaking he was too young to be employed, since you had to be sixteen in the State of New York to be allowed to work in agriculture. But since his parents realized how much their son was benefiting from being around the animals and generally playing farmer, they allowed him to go ahead and help out a little.

Not that Giles thought Mark would ever be a farmer, since his dad was a big shot in some online business, and his mom was a well-known socialite who would never be seen dead on a farm lest she soil her precious Louboutins or drop her Louis Vuitton purse in the mud. In fact, when the couple had first bought the piece of property next to Giles's farm, they had tried to shut him down and buy up the land so they could get rid of the stench, as they had explained it to the judge at the time.

They were essentially city folk who had decided that country life was what they wanted but hadn't realized that country life also includes farmers like Giles and his farm located right next to the piece of property they had bought, which incidentally had always been farmland before Farmer Cooper had died without any heirs, and the land had been sold to the Turners.

The Turners had lost their lawsuit, and the judge had even put them in their place and told them in no uncertain terms that when you want to live in the country, you have to take the good with the bad and not make a big fuss about a cock crowing at five o'clock in the morning, or the cows mooing when they need to be milked, or the pigs screeching, or the so-called stench of the manure, since it's all part and parcel of life in the countryside. And besides, the judge had told the indignant couple, if you really want to get rid of all the farmers, what are you going to eat? Or where do you think those pork chops are coming from, or those eggs or that milk your kid pours over his cornflakes in the morning? It all comes from those farmers you can't wait to shut down."

The couple had sobered up and realized they had gone too far, especially when the local community rallied around Giles and even launched a petition to drive the Turners out of town. Not exactly 'feathered and tarred,' but nevertheless it was clear that their initiative had made them deeply unpopular with the locals. To make amends and continue living there, the couple had to make reparations, even paying a visit to Giles at the farm and apologizing for what they had put him through. Over the years, he had developed an amicable relationship with Harry and Jessica, and especially with their son Mark, who had told his parents at the age of nine that he wanted to be a farmer just like Farmer Giles, much to their horror. Some people in town called it a form of poetic justice, but Giles didn't think the kid would actually become a farmer when all was said and done. However, five years had passed and Mark still seemed determined that farming was his future, so who knows? Maybe it would happen, and Giles would end up selling his farm to the kid so he could take over one day. Since he didn't have kids himself, he wouldn't mind if he did.

"What's wrong, Mark?" he asked now.

"It's Mom and Dad," Mark repeated, a horrified look in his eyes, the kind of look you sometimes see in the eyes of a victim of a traffic accident. "They're... " He gulped some more, then finally managed, "They're dead!" and promptly burst into loud sobs.

Giles's eyes now traveled down the kid's body, and he saw to his horror that his entire front was streaked with a dark red substance that could only be blood. Even his hands and shoes were covered in blood. He took hold of the kid, who was sobbing violently, and forced him to look into his eyes. "Mark, what happened? Tell me!"

The kid stopped sobbing long enough to say in broken tones, "I killed them, Giles. I killed my parents! I killed them both!"

CHAPTER 5

*A*fter the interrupted night we'd had, our first intention was to spend a lazy morning. We'd sleep in and then lounge about for a while doing absolutely nothing, and generally make up for the nap time we had missed last night. But of course, events intervened in the form of another interruption to the natural order of things. This time Uncle Alec didn't call his detective out of bed but decided to drop by the house in person. I'd just readjusted my position by snuggling up between Chase and Odelia and generally feeling on top of the world when all of a sudden the doorbell told me that my snuggles were at an end. Chase felt much the same way, for it was with a groan that he got out of bed and padded barefoot down the stairs, only clad in his boxer shorts, as is sometimes his habit. Lucky for us he doesn't sleep in the nude, as I don't think I would have the fortitude to deal with that type of contingency. Humans are weird enough to look at as it is, so I can't imagine having to look at them in the buff, as it were.

Moments later, the sound of Uncle Alec's voice drifted up the stairs, and so it didn't take long for Odelia to tie her long blond tresses behind her head in a ponytail, slip her feet into a pair of Hello Kitty slippers, pull on her bright pink dressing gown, and also head down the stairs. And since Dooley and I felt a little silly staying behind by our lonesome, we decided to follow suit.

When we arrived downstairs, Uncle Alec was standing wide-legged in the living room, indicating he had important information to share, since otherwise he would have been seated at the kitchen counter slurping from a cup of coffee and snacking on a glazed donut. In general, the atmosphere was a little subdued, I felt, and as I glanced up at our human to know what made it so, she said curtly, "There's been another family tragedy. This time a kid killed his mom and dad."

"A kid killed his parents?" I asked.

She nodded. "He confessed to a neighbor about what he did, and he was covered in blood, so there doesn't seem to be any doubt about what happened. We're going over there now. So if you want to join us, you're welcome, though there probably won't be much of an investigation as it's an open-and-shut case."

"The kid confessed," said her uncle. "So we placed him under arrest, even though he's a minor."

"How old is he?" asked Chase.

"Fourteen," said Uncle Alec, causing Chase to whistle through his teeth.

"My God."

"Yeah, you can say that again," said his superior officer.

And since time was of the essence, it didn't take long for our humans to get dressed and ready to head out. Dooley and I experienced a powerful sense of déjà vu when we crawled onto the backseat of Chase's pickup, and soon he was racing to the scene of the crime. He had turned on his police siren and his light bar on the roof so we could move through traffic like a knife through butter, which is always a pleasant experience.

"There seems to be an epidemic of family tragedies in town," said Dooley. "Last night, a father killed his wife and young son, and now a young boy killed his mom and dad. Do you think those two cases could be connected, Max?"

"I don't know, Dooley, but it seems highly unlikely. As it is, these things happen, sad though they may be, and people do sometimes lose control of themselves and do stupid things."

Odelia had turned to us and given us some background information on the couple who had been killed. Apparently, the man was a rich entrepreneur who had made his money creating online tools that could help boost productivity. This productivity suite had become very popular, and he had sold the company to a big conglomerate a couple of years ago and had decided to buy an old farm in Hampton Cove and fix it up. The farm was located right next to Farmer Giles's farm, and the couple had experienced a bumpy ride when they had first arrived, not taking as well as they would have expected to life in the country. But lately, things had settled down, and now they were an accepted and much-appreciated part of the local community, with the wife on several local committees and the couple donating generously to charity.

"Mom knows the woman quite well," she said now. "Or knew her well," she amended her statement. "She was a big patron of the library, and Mom met her occasionally, mostly when they arranged fundraisers for the library and other worthwhile causes. Once she organized an art exhibition at the library showcasing her own paintings, and Mom said they weren't bad. They all sold out, and the money went to the library."

The car was traversing large swathes of field, and I saw several cows gaping curiously at us, probably wondering what we were doing there. This was all Farmer Giles's land, and those cows were his, I knew. Before long, we were zooming through a gate, and moments later arrived at the house, which had been exquisitely renovated. It still resembled the old farm that once had stood there, but at least now it looked fit for a family to live there, whereas in the past it had fallen into disrepair after its owner had passed away with no relatives to leave the sprawling property to.

Police vehicles were parked haphazardly in the driveway, and before long we got out of the car and walked up to the main house. The crime scene people had come and gone, and so had the coroner, who had arranged for the bodies to be transported to the county coroner's office, where they would be subjected to a postmortem to determine the cause of death and ascertain whether the story Mark Turner had told his neighbor was true or not. According to the kid, he and his dad had developed a fractious relationship lately over the kid's future and how they each saw it. Mark wanted to become a farmer and had wanted to since the age of nine, but his father was vehemently against the idea and wanted him to go to college and get a business degree and enter the corporate world instead. His mom didn't have a fixed idea on the matter but was inclined to side with her husband. Over the years, they had gotten into arguments about the same topic, with Mark's parents taking the inflexible view that there simply wasn't any future in farming, and Mark insisting that's what he wanted to do with his life. But apparently this time that argument had ended with Mark grabbing a long knife out of a block of knives in the kitchen and sticking it into his dad's stomach. And when his mom entered the room and tried to take the knife off her son, he had also stuck it in her, though whether he had done it as a premeditated act or accidentally as a consequence of a struggle over the possession of the knife wasn't entirely clear yet, since Mark was suffering from a blackout and said he couldn't remember anything about what happened. All he knew was that when he woke up lying next to his parents' bodies, the knife was still in his hand and he was covered in their blood. He had panicked and run straight to his neighbor Giles.

Our job was to ascertain what had actually happened by talking to the family bulldog, who was traumatized, according to Odelia, and had sat catatonic in the corner of the room when the police got there, unwilling or unable to move from the spot. Apparently, he had witnessed the whole thing, and for now, the police had decided to leave him be and hadn't interfered with him at all.

It sounded like a tough assignment, I thought, especially since bulldogs are a very particular breed. Also, they aren't big fans of cats as far as I can tell. Still, if that was our mission, I felt it was incumbent upon us to carry it through to the bitter end. Especially since he was an eyewitness, so it was paramount we got him to talk.

"Maybe you should hire a dog whisperer," Dooley now suggested to Odelia. "You know, like a dog shrink? If this dog is seriously traumatized, he might need a shrink, not a pair of cats."

"Yeah, we might provoke him," I pointed out. "Bulldogs don't like cats all that much. Well, dogs in general, I guess. Unless they grew up with cats, they're not all that crazy about us."

"Just give it your best shot," our human said. "And then report back to me."

And since we'd been given our marching orders, Dooley and I set paw for the main house—there was also the old stable, which had been transformed into a garage for Mr. Parker's exclusive collection of cars—and walked in.

We found the bulldog where he had been sitting since the

tragedy happened, apparently. His name, according to Odelia, was Mooch, which I thought was a funny name for a dog. But then maybe the Turners had possessed a certain sense of humor when they named the dog. When I laid eyes on the creature, though, I immediately saw that the name was apt. It looked like a mooch, even though I had no idea what a mooch was.

Before we approached the dog, Dooley drew me aside. "So how do you want to play this, Max? Good cop, bad cop, maybe? With you playing the bad cop and me the good one?"

"I don't think now is the time to engage in such frivolities, Dooley," I said. "No games, just straight talk."

"I like that," said Dooley appreciatively. "Just give it to him straight. So do you want to do the talking, or should I lead with a question?"

"Let's just play this by ear," I suggested since I had absolutely no idea what to expect.

"Gotcha," he said, nodding. Then frowned. "Whose ear, Max? Yours or mine?"

"Let's just introduce ourselves and see what happens," I said.

And so we walked up to the dog. As we did, I couldn't help but notice a large pool of a dark crimson substance on the carpet, which could only be blood, and chalk outlines where the bodies of the parent pair had lain before being carried away. I shivered a little. After last night, this was the second time in twenty-four hours that we had been called to a murder scene.

But since we had a job to do, I decided to steel my resolve and get on with it. I plastered my most ingratiating smile onto my face and approached the bulldog, who was indeed lying in the corner of the room looking catatonic. He could have been one of those wax figures at Madame Tussaud's for the sense of life he displayed.

"Hi there Mooch—can I call you Mooch? My name is Max, and this is my friend Dooley. We would like to talk to you about what happened," I said.

The dog did not respond, didn't even deign to look up at us.

"We think it's very brave of you to stay here," Dooley added his two cents. "For what it's worth, we think it's terrible what happened, and we would like to offer you our assistance. Any way we can, anything you need. Just tell us, and we will probably be able to make it happen."

"Yeah," I said. "See that blond-haired woman over there? She's our human, and that big beefy guy over there? He's our human's husband. They both work for the police, and they're here to help find out what happened to your humans."

At this, a sort of sob escaped the bulldog's throat. Before long, he was quietly sobbing and blubbering.

"Was it something I said?" Dooley asked as he stared in amazement at the weeping dog.

"No, I think that the realization has hit him that his humans are no longer amongst us."

For a few moments, we simply let the dog come to terms with what was going on. But then, since we didn't have all the time in the world, I decided to continue the interview as best I could.

"So, would you be able to tell us in your own words what happened here, Mooch?" I asked. "And please take your time. We have all the time in the world."

But the dog shook his head. Clearly, he wasn't ready to talk to us yet. I would have handed him a tissue paper, but cats don't wear clothes, and as a consequence don't have pockets, so unfortunately I couldn't help him in that department. As it was, it wasn't necessary, as he simply licked his own tears from his face and made a couple of highly disturbing snorting sounds. The latter were so loud they made Odelia and Chase look up from their work and direct a worried glance in our direction. I gave them a reassuring sign that we had everything well in paw.

"It must be terrible to lose your humans like that," said Dooley, who had settled down next to the bulldog. "I can't imagine anything happening to our humans. I'd be devastated, to be honest. You, Max?"

"Mh? Oh, yeah, absolutely," I said. Just the thought of anything happening to Odelia or the rest of her family was enough to make me tear up myself. It was probably the worst that could happen to any pet. Apart maybe from discovering that your human has forgotten to run to the store and buy a fresh bag of kibble. Though in all honesty, those two events are probably not on the same scale. After all, kibble is replaceable, and humans generally aren't.

Finally, the dog seemed ready for speech. The first words out of his mouth surprised us a great deal, however. "Mark is innocent," he announced.

"What did you say?" I asked, sitting up a little straighter.

He cleared his throat. "Mark didn't do it. He didn't kill his parents."

"But... he confessed," I pointed out. "He told his neighbor how he killed them with a knife."

But the bulldog shook his head. "That's not what happened."

"So what did happen?" asked Dooley gently.

The dog glanced up at the ceiling while he uttered another mighty sob. "I don't know!" he finally lamented. "When it happened, I wasn't here. And I should have been here, to protect my humans. And I wasn't!"

"So where were you?" I asked.

He gave me a haunted look. "I was asleep," he said quietly. "And then when I woke up I decided to bury a bone."

"A bone?" asked Dooley. "But why would you bury it?"

"For later use," said the dog. "You never know who will sneak in and try to steal your bones, so you bury them where no one can find them, and then later when you want them, you simply dig them up again." He closed his eyes. "But why am I telling you this? You're cats, you don't understand."

"Oh, but we do," I assured him. "Of course we do. You bury a bone to make sure no other dogs can get at it. Very sound reasoning. Absolutely sound, I have to say."

As it was, I thought it was a little crazy to bury a bone and not consume it on the spot. But then I guess that's where cats and dogs differ. For one thing we're absolutely not interested in bones, which don't really hold a lot of nutrients, I would think, except maybe calcium. Though it could also be that dogs simply have a more powerful mauling machine in the form of their majestic maw, and cats don't. But be that as it may, I still wanted to get to the bottom of this story.

"So you were asleep, and then you buried your bone," I reiterated. "Presumably outside?"

"Yeah, out back," he said. "I have this spot where I bury all of my bones. Nobody will ever find them there, not even a passing dog. But anyway, by the time I was done burying this particular bone I heard this blood-curdling scream coming from the house, so I rushed over and was met with this scene from a horror movie. Mark was standing there, a knife in his hand, covered in blood, staring down at the inert and bloodied bodies of his parents."

"So... why would you say that he didn't do it?" I asked.

"Because I know Mark, all right? He's the sweetest kid in the world, and he would never do such a terrible thing. And also, he loved his parents. Even though he and his dad didn't always see eye to eye, there was a lot of love there, so he would never resort to violence to settle an argument."

"So there were arguments?" I probed.

"Of course there were. Mark is fourteen. What fourteen-year-old doesn't have arguments with his parents from time to time? But he didn't have a violent bone in his body."

"More bones," Dooley murmured with a knowing nod. "This case is all about bones."

"Is it true that they argued a lot about Mark's future?" I asked. "About him wanting to become a farmer and his dad not agreeing?"

"Yeah, lately they'd been arguing a lot about that. All the time, in fact. Mark wanted to work at the farm next door, and had been helping out there weekends and holidays. His folks liked that he had a fun hobby, but when he told them he wanted to make it his profession they told him in no uncertain terms that wasn't going to happen. They figured he was just a kid and what did he know. But I think Mark knew exactly what he wanted, and so maybe they should have listened more. But that still doesn't mean that he killed his parents, because he didn't."

"But you weren't here to see it," I said quietly.

The dog burst into loud sobs again. "I'll *never* dig up that bone!" he declared. "It will stay in the ground forever and ever, and I will *never* dig it up. As a punishment for myself for having neglected the primary duty a dog has: to protect his humans!" And he actually howled. Whether as a tribute to his late humans, or in protest to the investigation that seemed to have fingered Mark as the designated killer, I didn't know. What I did know was that it made everyone in the room stop whatever they were doing and stare at the strange trio: one big bulldog wailing away, one big-boned blorange cat and a fluffy small one. We truly were an incongruent trio, and they probably wondered if we had scratched Mooch to cause him to howl like that. But as it was, he suddenly stopped as abruptly as he had begun. And when I looked up, I saw that Chase was approaching us.

Mooch glanced up at the burly cop with an expectant

look on his face. Chase gave the dog a rub across the neck and behind his ears. "Good dog," he murmured affectionately. "You're a good dog, aren't you?"

"No, I'm not, detective," said Mooch. "I let down my humans, and now they're dead." And he hung his head and returned to his former catatonic state.

It was a testament to Chase's canine-loving attitude that he actually sat down next to Mooch and proceeded to softly talk to the dog, and before long, the dog had put his head in the cop's lap and was softly sniffling while Chase massaged his head.

Odelia's husband really was a dog person, I thought, since I couldn't remember him ever doing that with me. But it seemed to work, because gradually the dog became less anxious, and before long had closed his eyes and was gently snoring. For some reason, and don't ask me how I know this, I had a feeling that we'd see more of Mooch in the near future.

CHAPTER 6

Brutus woke up and for a moment wondered where he was. Then he saw the light streaming in through the window and remembered he was home, and relaxed. Lying on the bed which his humans had vacated, he stretched now and luxuriated in the sensation of having all of that space all to himself. Downstairs, noises from the kitchen told him that Marge and Tex were sitting down for breakfast along with Marge's mom, and he had to admit he loved those familiar sounds almost as much as he loved sitting down for breakfast himself, even though breakfast mostly consisted of kibble and some extras if Marge had taken the time to get out a nice snack for her cats.

Next to him, Harriet also stirred, and when she opened her eyes and gazed at him with those gorgeous green peepers of hers, he knew he was one of the luckiest cats in the world to have landed such amazing humans as well as the most gorgeous girlfriend in the history of the world.

"Hey, beautiful," he said. "Slept well?"

"Amazing," Harriet announced as she also stretched now

and yawned. "After cat choir, I was still thinking about the song I sang. Remember?"

"How could I forget?" he said. Harriet had enchanted all of them with a perfect rendition of a Bruce Springsteen song, surprising everyone since usually she liked to tackle favorite singers like Céline. But Bruce? No way. But she had done a pretty great job, and had left her audience mesmerized, not just by the way she had chosen to interpret the song, but especially by the sheer power her voice projected. Almost as if she could reach the moon and the stars with her voice. He wasn't sure if she had managed quite such a feat, but at the very least she had reached their neighbors, who had all fallen over themselves to lean out of their respective windows and hurl their favorite footwear through the air in their direction. Just another way to show their appreciation. Some humans like to applaud after a great performance, others throw shoes.

"So what happened to Max and Dooley?" asked Harriet. "They weren't at cat choir last night, and when we got back, they weren't home either."

"No, I noticed the same thing," said Brutus. But then Odelia and Chase hadn't been home either, and Gran had been Grace's designated babysitter again.

"Probably some case they were called away for," Harriet said.

Brutus's good mood diminished to some extent as he experienced a pang of guilt. "Maybe we should have tagged along," he said. "Instead of going to cat choir, I mean."

"We didn't know," said Harriet simply. "So we couldn't possibly have tagged along to whatever case they were called away for. And besides, I'm sure they're fine. Max can handle the odd case from time to time. And if he does need our assistance, I'm sure he'll ask us."

"Yeah, I guess so," said Brutus. Max was a good detective,

and if he did need their help with some of the pawwork, he wasn't shy about enlisting it.

And so they decided that maybe it was time for them to start their day, and they both got out of bed and gracefully tripped down the stairs to join the rest of the family. Grace was also there, which meant that Odelia and Chase had probably been called away on a case early. Or maybe they were still out from last night, which meant that whatever this case might be, it was something pretty serious.

"So what's going on?" he asked.

Gran looked up from her breakfast, which consisted of oatmeal this morning. "Murder case," she said curtly. "A kid killed his mom and dad. And last night there was another murder case. This one a murder-suicide where some guy killed his wife and son and then himself." She shook her head. "Bad business in both cases."

"Did you know any of the people involved?" asked Brutus.

"I didn't, but Marge did. Right, Marge? You knew the Turners?"

"Yeah, I did," Marge confirmed. She was sipping from a cup of coffee, as fond of the hot brew as her daughter. "Jessica Turner organized a fundraiser for the library last year that netted us a lot of funds. And she dropped by the library from time to time to help out. She was a great friend of mine, and I'll miss her terribly." She made a face. "I just can't believe Mark would do such a thing. He accompanied her once or twice when she dropped by, and he always struck me as such a nice and well-mannered kid."

"Those are the worst," Gran insisted. "They look like the sweetest kids on the planet, but underneath, they're vicious little psychos. I'll bet that he's been torturing rabbits and squishing ants since the moment he could walk."

"Is that why Odelia and Chase were out of bed so early

this morning?" asked Tex as he folded his newspaper and placed it on the table.

"Yeah, Alec got the call first," said Marge. "And then he called Chase and Odelia out of bed this morning."

"The kid actually confessed," said Gran. "Told a neighbor about what he'd done." She shook her head. "I hope they throw the book at the nasty little brute."

"Ma, he's only fourteen," said Marge. "And besides, I'm sure it's not as cut-and-dried as it looks. Maybe he had his reasons to do what he did."

"His reasons!" said Gran. "He murdered his mom and dad in cold blood! Stuck a big kitchen knife into them and left them to die!"

Tex glanced down at the kitchen knife that was lying on the table and moved it out of reach of his mother-in-law. "Let's just wait and see what Odelia has to say before we make any judgments," was his advice. "In my experience, these things are never as straightforward as they seem."

"He confessed! He told his neighbor that he killed them!"

"All I'm saying is that things are often not what they seem," Marge argued. She got up from the table. "I'm going to take a shower. Unless either of you needs to go first?"

But her mom and her husband shook their heads, and so Marge got first dibs on the bathroom.

"I would like to take a shower," Grace piped up. She had been sitting quietly at the breakfast table, munching on a cheese sandwich. But of course, the grownups couldn't understand her. Only Brutus and Harriet could, for some reason.

"Grace wants to take a shower," Brutus said helpfully, but Gran decided to ignore him while she surfed on her phone. On the other side of the table, Tex was also surfing on his phone, and for a few moments, no one spoke.

"Why don't I get a smartphone?" Grace lamented. "I also would like to check my messages."

Brutus and Harriet laughed at this. "Who would send you messages?" asked Harriet.

"My friends," said the toddler without missing a beat. "I meet a lot of people at daycare, you know, and I'm sure if we all had phones, we would communicate all the time."

"But you don't even know how to read or write yet," Harriet pointed out.

Grace shrugged. "So? With a smartphone, you don't need to know how to read or write. You dictate the messages you want to send, and you get your phone to read the messages you receive. Easy peasy. This world is made for people like me: the little people. And reading and writing is no requirement at all."

"She's probably right," said Brutus. "Nowadays, you probably don't need to go to school anymore. Anything you want to know, you can find online. Kids don't need to memorize any dates because they can look them up. They don't need math since they can ask their phone to make the calculations, and they don't need geography, biology, physics, history, or any of the other stuff they teach in school. All they need to know is on their phones."

"I very much doubt whether that's the case, snuggle bear," said Harriet. "There's still a ton of stuff you need to learn if you want to find your way in life."

"Like what? Pretty soon now, computers will take over from humans and will do all the jobs. Humans will become completely superfluous and will eventually cease to exist since they no longer will be necessary. Cats will still exist, since cats can't be replaced by a computer."

"I guess so," said Harriet dubiously, trying to find the flaw in his reasoning, which he knew she couldn't since he was right.

"Humans will still exist," said Grace, "even after computers have taken over. Because humans can give you cuddles, and computers can't."

Now that was true enough, Brutus had to admit. At least here was one thing humans could do that computers couldn't. Though it wouldn't surprise him if they invented a cuddle robot soon that would give even better cuddles than an actual human.

Before long, Marge returned, a towel wrapped around her head, and then it was Tex's turn to use the bathroom and then Gran's. It was a daily morning ritual that Brutus enjoyed very much. For some reason, and he didn't know why, it gave him a sense of happiness to see their humans go through these rituals. Even Grace seemed to like it, for she was directing a gummy smile at her grandmother. The latter picked her up from her chair and placed her squarely on her lap. For a few moments, grandmother and granddaughter 'talked' and then Grace announced that she wanted Harriet and Brutus to accompany her to daycare today. At which point Brutus pointed out that cats weren't allowed in the daycare Grace was at, since not all the kids there even liked cats, and also it probably wasn't safe, since not all kitties were as well-behaved as they were. Grace pouted for a moment before relenting. She really was a great kid, Brutus thought, and a credit to the family.

Which is when Grace's parents walked in through the kitchen door, accompanied by Max and Dooley, completing the band. Before long, the humans were telling their fellow humans about the morning they'd had, and Max and Dooley were telling their feline friends. So when a large bulldog waddled in and blinked at the collected company, who all stared back at him with a look of surprise, Brutus and Harriet had already been warned.

His name was Mooch, and for the time being he was

going to be their new housemate. At least until some other arrangements could be made, since his human was in prison for murdering his parents. And even though minors couldn't be convicted like adults could, there would probably be consequences for what Mark Turner had done, and those consequences would also affect Mooch.

"Mooch, meet the family," said Dooley, doing the honors. "Family, meet Mooch."

And that's how their strictly feline company was expanded with a canine. Maybe, Brutus thought, he shouldn't have gotten out of bed that morning. And just like that, his mellow and pleasant mood gave way to one of annoyance. It wasn't that he disliked dogs, because he didn't. But somehow he could foresee a host of problems connected to this sudden and unexpected introduction of the canine element into a strictly feline household.

And for some reason, he blamed Max.

CHAPTER 7

The plot, which had seemed so straightforward the previous night, thickened when the news reached us that Paul Römer, the man who had murdered his family, had robbed a Seven-Eleven the night before. And not one Seven-Eleven but several, and some other convenience stores and also two gas stations and a night shop. Apparently, he'd been fairly amateurish in the way he had carried out these crimes because he'd been positively identified not only by the people he had robbed, but also because he was caught on camera in all of the places he had held up.

The different reports of last night's hold-ups trickled into the station one by one, and by the time eleven o'clock rolled around, Chase had a pretty good idea of how Mr. Römer had spent the evening. He'd started on his nocturnal marathon at ten o'clock with the hold-up of his first Seven-Eleven on Parker Street and had gone from strength to strength over the course of the next couple of hours, until he had hit his twelfth store and decided to call it a night. At which point he'd returned home with the loot and had proceeded to murder his family and also himself.

It simply did not make sense, Chase thought. Unless, of course, he had gotten into a fight with his wife over his criminal activities, and they had argued, and he'd lost his temper. But by all accounts, Paul Römer had not been a violent man, and from what his neighbors had told them, the couple had seemed harmonious enough. Loving, even after ten years of marriage. And then, of course, there was the fact that he had also opted to murder his own son. He may have lost his temper after a fight with his wife, but why kill the boy?

There was something very strange about this case. Something that simply did not add up. He went over the different elements in his mind, sitting back in his chair behind his desk at the police station, his eyes closed. The cats had reported that one of the neighboring pets had heard a woman scream. This was around seven-thirty, so long before Römer had set about his raid of convenience stores and gas stations. This same pet had also heard a male voice beseech an unknown second party, 'Please don't leave me.' It could have been Römer, of course, and it was possible that his wife had announced that she was leaving him for some reason that they didn't know about.

Then there was the fact that the Römer kid was sick. A relative had told them that he suffered from a rare form of kidney cancer, and the doctors didn't think he had long to live. There was a treatment the Römers had been looking into, but it was an experimental one in a private Swiss clinic and it was prohibitively expensive, which might explain why Mr. Römer had decided to become a criminal and rob all of those places in one night. But he must have known that he was going to be caught, and very quickly, too, or else he would have worn a mask at least.

So the guy wants to collect money to pay for his kid's cancer treatment and robs a bunch of stores. Then he arrives home with the loot and murders his family instead? Chase opened his eyes and rubbed them. Nothing about this case made sense. And now he had a second case on his desk, which also didn't make a lot of sense to him. Mark Turner, who had murdered his mom and dad, and according to the bulldog he couldn't have done it.

He grimaced. How had he suddenly become a pet detective? A detective who considered the testimonial of pets as important or even crucial to his investigations? It all seemed a little outside the realm of the acceptable to him, and he shared this view with his boss, who also didn't like all this meddling of cats and dogs and whatever other species into what should be simple and straightforward police inquiries. But since Odelia was the kind of person she was, and possessed this unique gift, he couldn't very well discount the introduction into his police detective work of the pet element, no matter how strange it might seem to an outsider. Good thing none of his other colleagues were au courant, or otherwise he would probably find himself out of a job posthaste.

A knock at the door brought him out of his reverie, and when the door opened, he saw that his chief had joined him. "And? Any progress to report?" asked the boss.

He shook his head. "Just that I find the whole Römer business far from the cut-and-dry case we thought it was last night, Chief," he said. "And the same thing applies to the Turner case, if I'm honest. I mean, we talked to the kid's schoolteachers, his principal, fellow students, and they had nothing but great things to say about him. Hardworking, clever, intelligent, but also friendly and essentially a sweet kid. And suddenly he turns around and murders his parents in cold blood?"

"Not in cold blood," the Chief pointed out as he lowered his right buttock on the edge of his detective's desk. "He and his old man got into an argument, things got heated, and he stabbed him. It happens, Chase. Even to sweet kids like Mark Turner. They can also get triggered and lose their temper." He quirked an eyebrow. "Whatever the bulldog says."

Chase grimaced. "He's living with us now, you know. I decided to take him home with us for the time being, since no one else seems to be interested in having him."

"No relatives?"

He shook his head. "Harry Turner's sister lives in Canada and she's already expressed a fervent wish not to adopt the dog since she claims she's allergic to pets. And Jessica Turner's sister is in Mexico right now on vacation and didn't seem all that excited about adopting Mooch either."

"Funny name, Mooch," said the chief with a grin.

"Yeah, it is," said Chase with a warm smile as he thought back to the bulldog. "He's such a great dog, and you should have seen his face. He looked so sad."

"You've got a big heart, buddy," said the Chief. "Though I can't imagine Odelia's cats being happy about the sudden arrival of a dog in their midst."

"Oh, they're not happy at all," said Chase. "But she explained to them it's only for the time being until we can find him a new home. Though from what Vesta told me, it's not easy placing dogs like Mooch. People love to adopt pups and kittens, but older dogs like Mooch, and especially dogs that have lived through trauma like this, are not very popular. And also, we need to make sure that the people who do adopt him will treat him with the love that he deserves."

"I have a feeling Mooch may be with you much longer than you anticipate." He turned serious. "Okay, so about the Römer case. What's the story on these hold-ups?"

And so he told the story to his superior officer, who agreed with him that the case didn't meet the smell test, and advised him to dig a little deeper to find out what was really going on. As far as Mark Turner was concerned, that was for the judge to decide. They had made a legitimate arrest, had a written confession from the kid, and so that case was closed. Chase didn't fully agree with this assessment, but he could understand where the Chief was coming from, and frankly speaking couldn't argue with the decision since he didn't have other elements to add that would either disprove Mark's version of events or shed a new light on things.

And so he grabbed his coat, and a moment later was on his way to the *Gazette* offices to tell his wife that if she could spare the time, and if her boss would let her, they had a case to sink their teeth into—the case of the family man who mysteriously had decided one evening to take the lives of his entire family.

* * *

DOOLEY and I were sleeping soundly and pleasantly, basking in the atmosphere of absolute quiet that often reigns in Odelia's office when, all of a sudden, the door opened and Chase came barging in. He seemed to direct a look at us that can only be termed 'expectant,' and I got the impression that our nice sojourn was already at an end. I hadn't slept well last night for obvious reasons and had even had to forgo that pleasant pastime of cat choir because of the case that had been thrown in our laps. And now I had a feeling that the case would cause us to lose even more sleep. For Odelia got up and said, "Let's go, Max and Dooley. Time to go and talk to those turtles again. Or was it a Chihuahua?"

"Both," I said sadly. For some reason, I didn't look forward to making Rita and Ralph's further acquaintance. I'd seen them steadily and I'd seen them whole and had decided that I didn't want to see any more of them. But if Odelia thought there was some benefit to be derived from our prolonged association with these turtles, I couldn't think of a good reason why we shouldn't.

As it turned out, Paul Römer had displayed some very unusual and concerning behavior the night before. Before morphing into a murderer, he had also decided to try his hand at robbing gas stations and Seven-Elevens. Possibly these were things that were on his bucket list. Or the experience hadn't been as exhilarating as he'd hoped, and so he had decided to become a murderer instead.

It wasn't an explanation I found entirely satisfying, and clearly neither Odelia nor Chase did either, and so we were ushered from our cozy little nook and into Chase's car for some more investigating. I could have told Odelia that she didn't need us for this investigation, but then I would have come across as utterly and completely ungrateful, so I didn't. Instead, Dooley and I both vowed to put our best paw forward and give satisfaction as much as we could. Even if it meant a renewed association with the turtles.

We arrived at the cul-de-sac and were greeted with a police presence still present at the house, which is customary under the circumstances, and as we pulled to a stop, a woman came out of the house where Mike and Mikaela Campbell lived, as their surname turned out to be, and I thought that she was quite possibly the lady of the house. I had heard her last night but hadn't actually laid eyes on her. And so when she addressed Chase and Odelia, I immediately recognized the voice.

"How long are you people going to be here?" she asked.

"It depends on the state of the investigation," said Chase carefully. Most people hate it when the police stick around and outstay their welcome.

But Mrs. Campbell's face morphed into a big smile. "I hope you stay forever," she said. "Since you people have been here, those annoying punks have stayed away. And if you stick around for another week or so, they might never return and find themselves a different street to terrorize."

"These would be the hooligans you referred to last night, ma'am?" asked Chase as he got out his notebook.

"Yeah, about a dozen kids who race up and down the street on motorcycles, kick over trash containers, spray graffiti on the walls of our houses, call us all kinds of horrible names, and even push over old Mrs. Flower from three doors down. We had to call an ambulance that time, which they wouldn't allow to pass, and then they tried to set fire to the ambulance and also picked a fight with one of the paramedics and threw rocks at the poor man as he tried to put Mrs. Flower on a stretcher. They're horrible kids, and I hope they never come back."

"I've read the police reports," Chase told her. "And we have sent a car to patrol the street."

"I know, but each time you're gone, they come back. And I understand that you can't put an officer here twenty-four-seven, but maybe you could at least arrest some of these kids and put them behind bars for a while. Maybe then they'll learn the lesson."

"Or they might return to take revenge," Odelia pointed out.

Mikaela nodded. "I know you're right. But what else can we do? Unless you want us to turn into vigilantes and take the law into our own hands?"

"No, we certainly don't encourage that," said Chase quickly as he held up his hands to stave off the suggestion. "What we would like to see is for this gang of street kids to remove themselves from the territory of Hampton Cove entirely. Mostly they're not even from around here. Most of them are from neighboring towns, where the mayors and the police have made life too hard for them, so they decided to relocate and come here."

"Which is an admission that you're too soft on them, right?" said Mikaela smartly.

Chase grimaced. "We'll find a way to deal with them, Mrs. Campbell. Trust me. But for now, we're focusing on the investigation into the death of the Römers. Have you remembered anything since we talked last night?"

"Um…" Her face brightened. "Yes, I did remember something. When we went to bed last night I locked the back door, but when I came down for a glass of water it was unlocked. The lock hadn't been tampered with as far as I could tell, but the door was open. I don't know if that's in any way significant, but I just thought I'd tell you."

"Was anything stolen?"

She shook her head as she drew her nightgown closer around her person. "I don't think so. But that doesn't mean there wasn't someone in the house. They could also have planted something, since these kids are into dealing drugs, and so maybe they plant stuff in houses when they're afraid of being picked up by the police. I've read about this kind of stuff, you know."

"It's possible," Chase allowed. "But highly unlikely they would select your house. Mostly they pick houses of people they know, friends who haven't been in contact with the police. Not total strangers."

"Could you check if anything was taken?" asked Odelia. "Just to make sure."

"I will," said Mikaela.

And as the woman returned to her house, Odelia gave me and Dooley a look of significance. I have to say we followed Mikaela with dragging paws, and it gave me very little satisfaction having to interview those turtles all over again. But she seemed to think their statement contained elements that might be important, and so to go over them again was probably a good idea.

This is how Dooley and I found ourselves entering the Turner backyard once again, looking left and right to ascertain that Mikaela or Mike weren't there, and going in search of Rita and Ralph. We found them sunning on a flat stone at the back of the garden, next to a small pond the Turners had constructed there for the benefit of their turtles. It was very thoughtful of them, I thought.

The moment Rita saw us, she smiled and said, "Oh, there you are. I was wondering if you'd be back."

"Criminals always return to the scene of the crime," said Ralph, who didn't seem as happy about our return as his wife did.

"Ralph, don't be like that," said Rita. "Tom and Nolan are nice, upstanding cats."

"Max," I corrected her. "Max and Dooley."

"Just tell us what you want," Ralph grumbled.

"Well, news has reached our ears that Paul Römer robbed no less than twelve stores last night—convenience stores and gas stations and such. So the police are obviously wondering if this was his first time, or if it was a regular habit of his. You know, like a hobby if you will."

"Oh, so he went and did it, did he?" said Rita, shaking her head sadly. "What you have to know about Paul is that he was crazy about his little boy, and when Hector got sick, he was understandably devastated. So he probably went a little crazy trying to find a way to save his life. And they did find a clinic that was testing an experimental cure for the type of disease he was suffering from, but it cost more than the Römers could afford. Which is probably why he came up with the plan to rob those stores."

"How do you know all that?" I asked, marveling at the information this turtle had in her possession. And also wondering why she hadn't told us last night.

"Oh, I overheard them talking about it," said Rita simply.

"I spend a lot of time out here, you see, and so did the Römers. Well, they in their backyard, and I in mine, of course. But everything they discussed I could hear loud and clear."

And here I thought she was hard of hearing. Apparently not *that* hard of hearing!

"That's very interesting," I said.

"Why, thanks," she said brightly. "I aim to please."

"Oh, God," Ralph muttered.

"And so when Paul told his wife that the only way to save Hector was to rob a bunch of stores, at first she wasn't convinced, but in the end she agreed that it was probably the only way."

CHAPTER 8

We met up with our humans again when they were on the verge of knocking on the door of the Römers' other neighbor, the one that didn't own a pet. Her name was Alice Morgan, according to Odelia, and she was next on their list of people to talk to. All of these neighbors in the cul-de-sac had been paid a visit last night by either Chase or Odelia or one of Uncle Alec's officers, but apparently Chase felt it necessary to talk to them again, in more depth this time, as he wasn't satisfied with their initial findings, now that Mr. Römer's bizarre nocturnal raid had come to light.

The door opened, and a petite lady appeared, who gazed at the collected company on her doorstep with some surprise. "Oh, you're back," she said, and her words lacked the ring of happy anticipation. She didn't invite us in, and I had the impression the interview would be conducted on her doorstep.

"So we looked into the case involving your neighbors the Römers a little more," said Chase, taking the lead, "and as important information has come to light, we would like to ask you a few more questions."

"Shoot," she said curtly but without much enthusiasm.

"Paul Römer went on an armed-robbery spree last night, targeting at least a dozen convenience stores and gas stations that we know of. You knew the Römers well, having lived next to them for the past ten years, so would you say that type of behavior comes as a surprise to you?"

She stared at the cop, then blinked. "Paul robbed convenience stores?"

"He did. A dozen of them, and gas stations. He didn't bother wearing a mask, so it wasn't hard to identify him. He was caught on CCTV, and the store clerks easily recognized him when we showed them Paul's picture."

"My God," said the woman, becoming a little more animated. "No, I wouldn't say that kind of behavior was typical for Paul. In fact, it was completely out of character for him. He was a decent man, you know, not a gangster. Always polite, well-dressed, friendly and kind. The perfect neighbor, really. So why..." She thought for a moment. "It's true that they were desperate to lay their hands on a great deal of money. For Hector, you know. He had a disease, and they were hoping to travel to this clinic in Switzerland to get him treated. But it was going to cost them a lot of money. Money that they didn't have."

"Couldn't they have mortgaged their house?"

"I'm pretty sure they did. But it still wasn't enough." She shook her head. "But to go and rob a bunch of stores. That really surprises me. Did he... shoot anyone?"

"Nobody got injured," said Chase. "He used the same gun he later turned on his family and on himself, but he didn't fire a single shot during this robbery spree. The last store he hit was around two o'clock last night, at which point he returned home."

"Well, like I told you last night, I never heard anything. No shots fired, nothing. But then I sleep very soundly. I take Benadryl, you see, and that really knocks me out. And also, we don't share a common wall. There's about six feet between these houses, so in general I don't hear what goes on next door. The same goes for my other neighbors, Raquel and Rafe Williams. Though they get really loud sometimes, and when they do, I can hear some of it."

"So about these kids, Mrs. Morgan," said Odelia, taking over. "Did you see them last night?"

Alice Morgan shook her head. "I didn't see them. That doesn't mean they weren't there, of course. I spent all evening in my backyard, weeding, so if they were out there, up to their usual tricks, I wouldn't have seen them."

"But you would have heard them, right? Since they're usually pretty loud, racing up and down the street on their motorcycles?"

"Yeah, I guess you're right. If they had been here I would have heard them. Though sometimes they just hang out, you know. They pick a spot and then don't move away from it for hours. Which is pretty annoying, since I don't like to pass by them, as I'm afraid they'll start calling me names or harassing me. Like they did with Mrs. Flower last week. They actually shoved her and she broke her hip, the poor woman. And then when the ambulance came they even threw rocks at the poor paramedics and tried to block the ambulance from leaving. The police had to come and escort the ambulance and make sure they could get Mrs. Flower to the hospital."

"Yeah, we heard about that," said Chase.

"Sometimes they even trample all over our backyards at night, stomping around and destroying our lovely flowers. Just the other day I woke up in the morning and all of my flower beds had been flattened. As if some big giant had been drunkenly trampling around." Mrs. Alice Morgan gave Chase a hard look. "You should be doing something about it, detective. Make sure those kids are off the street and stop bothering and molesting innocent people like us and Mrs. Flower. Who's going to pay for the hospital? Those kids should be in jail, and their parents forced to pay Mrs. Flower's bills. It's simply a disgrace the way the police are letting us all down."

I understood now where Alice Morgan's cold attitude towards the police was coming from. Like the other neighbors on this cul-de-sac, she felt let down by them in the way they allowed these young punks to ruin their lives.

"We are looking into that," Chase assured her. "So back to the Römers. Is there anything else you can tell us about last night? Anything you noticed while you were out there weeding?"

Mrs. Morgan thought for a moment, then finally shook her head. "I heard Maria and Paul out back talking, but nothing special was said that I can remember. Though I have to say I wasn't paying all that much attention. I'm not a busybody, you know. I don't stick my nose in other people's business, and I expect them not to stick their noses in mine. That way I don't get in bad with anybody."

"Do some of the other neighbors here take a different view?" asked Odelia keenly.

Alice smiled. "You mean, are there any nosey parkers amongst my neighbors? Absolutely. The nosiest parker is probably Raquel Williams and her husband Rafe." She gestured with her head to the house where Fifi lived. "There's nothing those two don't know about the people that live here, including me, I'm afraid to admit. Raquel is such a charming person you can't help but tell her stuff about yourself, even though you vowed not to. She has this open, disarming way about her that instantly makes you feel like she's your best friend."

"Yeah, I know people like that," Odelia said. "You tell them stuff that you later regret."

"Exactly!" said Mrs. Morgan. "And then she turns around and inserts little tidbits about what you told her in confidence to your other neighbors, and at the end of the day, your private stuff is spread all around the neighborhood. And you can't even fault her for it because you're the one who blabbed about it in the first place." She shook her head. "I'm much more careful now, though. When I first moved here, I was so happy when I met Raquel. I really thought I'd made a friend, you know. It took me a couple of months before I realized that everything I told her was passed on, and that I had to watch what I said to her."

"Okay, so you've told us what kind of a man Paul Römer was," said Chase, consulting his little notebook. "But you haven't told us about Mrs. Römer."

"Maria? Oh, she was just the sweetest, gentlest soul imaginable. The kind of person you could always bother for a cup of rice or sugar, you know. I know it sounds like a cliché, but she didn't have a nasty bone in her body. Sometimes I thought she was a little too naive for her own good. You know when they say about a person how they're too good for this world? Well, Maria was that kind of person. Too good for this world, and also for this neighborhood. Like this one time I told her she shouldn't be so open with Raquel, and she just stared at me with those big blue eyes of hers, as if I'd said the most outrageous thing. She couldn't see the bad in people, only the good. And I think sometimes it bit her in the ass."

"In what way?" asked Odelia.

She thought for a moment. "There was this one time when we were all together at the annual summer picnic, and Maria had made these amazing chocolate chip cookies? They were really to die for, and she had made plenty, she thought, enough for the whole neighborhood. But one hour in, she saw they were all gone, which surprised her since she had spent all night and had really baked a ton. Later I had to help Raquel carry the big bowl of fruit punch out of their house and onto the little roundabout here, where we organize our picnics, and I couldn't help but notice how stacks of Maria's cookies were lying in plastic boxes on their kitchen counter. And I know they were Maria's because she had made them really big, in a very distinct shape. So I asked Raquel about it, and she said she had made them for the school bake sale."

"So she was selling Maria's cookies?"

Alice nodded. "She actually had the gall to steal Maria's cookies and then pass them off as her own while she sold them at the school bake sale. Talk about brazen. But when I told Maria about it, she simply shrugged it off. She said I was probably mistaken and Raquel was using the same recipe, which was impossible since Maria's recipe had been handed down from her grandmother to her mother and then to her. So those cookies were absolutely unique." She glanced over to her left for a moment, and a sad look came into her eyes. "I'll miss them, you know. Especially Maria. She was such a lovely person. Possibly the nicest and sweetest person I've ever met in my life."

Chase thanked her for her time and promised that he would look into this business of the neighborhood punks, and Alice said she'd hold him to his promise. For a moment, we stood on the sidewalk, and then it was time to meet Raquel, the alleged chocolate chip cookie thief, and her husband Rafe. And for Dooley and me to make Fifi's acquaintance again. Though, frankly speaking, I didn't really see the point since there's a big difference between stealing cookies and murdering an entire family in cold blood.

Which is why I asked Odelia what the point of these interviews was. "I thought it was obvious that Paul Römer had killed his wife and son?" I asked. "So why are you interviewing all of their neighbors again?"

"Because something doesn't make sense," she said. "Why hit a bunch of convenience stores so you can raise money for your boy's operation, only to arrive home and shoot him? Something doesn't add up, Max."

"No," I said as I gave this some thought. "I guess it doesn't." Though it was always possible that the money that Paul had collected on his raid wasn't sufficient to pay for the treatment, and that the couple had been at their wit's end. "So was the money from the raid found at the house?" I asked.

She turned to her husband and posed the question, but Chase shook his head. "Nothing was found, so we assume that Paul, before returning home after his raid, decided to hide the money somewhere in case the police came looking. That way, Maria could pick up the money if Paul was arrested and fly off to Switzerland with Hector on her own. At least that's what we assume happened. We're now looking into possible hiding places where he could have stashed the loot, but so far we haven't found it yet."

He pressed his finger to the buzzer of the Williams place, and immediately loud barking told us that at least Fifi was home. Moments later, the door opened and an extremely bronzed woman stood before us. Her skin looked like leather, and I would have pegged her in her early fifties. Her hair was a perfect blond and her face made up to perfection. All in all, she reminded me a little bit of a mannequin.

She blinked in surprise, then plastered a big smile on her face. "Oh, detectives!" she caroled. "Am I glad to see you! Come on in. I've just baked a fresh batch of chocolate chip cookies, and you can be the first ones to taste them!"

CHAPTER 9

We met Fifi in the kitchen looking smug. And when I glanced in the direction of her food bowls, it immediately became clear why: her bowls were all filled to the rim with some delicious-smelling stuff, and as my nostrils took in those delicious smells, I felt inexorably drawn to those bowls. But before I could take a step in their direction, Fifi was arresting me with a forbidding look.

"No way, buddy," she said in a low sort of tone. "That's mine."

"I was just—"

"Uh-uh."

"But I wasn't actually going to—"

"Mine," she said emphatically.

I sighed in defeat. "Oh, fine."

"That smells so delicious," said Dooley, who had missed the exchange. "Can I have a sniff?"

Fifi rolled her eyes. "Oh, for crying out loud. No, you can't take a sniff. Do I come into your home and start sniffing at your food? No, I do not. Because I'm a dog who's well aware of the social niceties and I don't do that kind of thing. And since this is my home and you're simply guests here, I expect you to behave accordingly, is that understood?"

"Perfectly," I said. Though I have to say that the smell of Fifi's food combined with the amazing smell of those freshly baked chocolate chip cookies was almost too powerful to resist. A lesser cat would simply have shoved that little Chihuahua out of the way and attacked those bowls, social niceties be damned. But since I am essentially a well-behaved cat, I resisted the overwhelming urge to give Fifi a piece of my mind—or a close-up of my well-developed right paw.

"And?" said Raquel Williams. "What do you think? Pretty tasty, huh?"

"These are good," said Chase, his mouth full of cookie. "Really good."

I would have thought that he would have declined, claiming he never ate chocolate chip cookies while on duty, but clearly such a rule didn't exist in the Hampton Cove PD rule book. Instead, he took a second cookie when offered, straight from the cookie sheet.

"Your own recipe?" asked Odelia innocently as she nibbled from her own cookie. She ate like a mouse, I thought, but then she usually did.

"Absolutely," said Raquel. "Handed down from my mom, who got it from her mom, and so on down the generations. A real family tradition, these chocolate chip cookies."

"Maria Römer was famous for *her* chocolate chip cookies," Odelia continued. "I wish I'd had a chance to taste them, as apparently they were delicious."

"They weren't bad," said Raquel. "But not as good as mine, obviously. I asked her once, and she said she got the recipe from a YouTube video." She grimaced as she held up her hands. "She should have asked me. I would have gladly shared my recipe. I even offered her, but she said she wasn't interested." She smiled her radiant smile again. "Another cookie, detective?"

Chase, who was already on his third cookie, and had seemingly forgotten all about the reason we were there in the first place, now pulled himself together. "If you don't mind, we would like to ask you a few more questions about last night, Mrs. Williams."

"Raquel, please. And can I call you Chase?"

"Um..."

"Okay, so we would like to go over the events of last night, Mrs. Williams," said Odelia, taking over from her chocoholic husband. She glanced around. "Your husband isn't home?"

"No, Rafe is in New Jersey. He's a sales rep for a consumer goods company so he visits a lot of stores. Supermarkets and such. He should be back tomorrow."

"He wasn't home last night either?"

Raquel shook her head. "He's often away on business, but I've got Fifi to keep me company."

Fifi beamed at this, and I couldn't blame her. It's always nice to be needed.

"Okay, so reports have come in that Paul Römer robbed a number of convenience stores before he returned home. You've been his neighbor for ten years now?"

"Something like that," said Raquel.

"So, would you associate that kind of behavior with your neighbor?"

"Paul robbed a convenience store?"

"A dozen of them," said Chase, wiping the crumbs from his fingers.

"My God. No, I wouldn't say that's Paul Römer. If anything, it sounds more like the kind of thing those hooligans who've been terrorizing this neighborhood for the past three months would do. Paul was an upstanding citizen. He was a manager at our local branch of Capital First Bank, you know. A very distinguished figure, always dressed to the nines in a suit and tie, out of the door at seven in the morning, clutching his briefcase, and home by six. A real stickler for routine, that one." She made a face. "We had them over from time to time, Maria and Paul, and he liked things just so. His steak had to be medium rare, his vegetables not too mushy but also not too crispy. The right wine with dinner, his napkin placed just so. Very nitpicky. And frankly impossible to live with. I remember telling Rafe after they left that if he was like Paul, I would have thrown him out on his ear a long time ago." She laughed a throaty laugh. "Lucky for me, Rafe is just about the opposite of Paul in every respect. Not that he's messy or anything, but he's definitely not a big stick-in-the-mud like Paul." She then held a hand to her mouth. "I probably shouldn't have said that. Don't speak ill of the dead and all that. But you asked me what Paul was like, so I told you. That's not wrong of me, is it?"

"No, it's not," said Chase. "In fact, it's exactly what we're looking for as we try to build a picture of what Mr. Römer and his wife were like."

"Oh, she was all right, I guess," said Raquel, who seemed to enjoy this conversation immensely. "A little spineless and basically a goody two shoes, but the harmless sort. Exactly the type of person you'd expect in the suburbs, really. Kissing her husband goodbye every morning when he left for work, spending her days taking care of their perfect little boy and making sure the house looked spic and span, and welcoming hubby home in the evening with a home-cooked meal on the table." She made a face of disgust. "At first, I thought she was putting on a show, but it was all too real. The perfect housewife, a transplant from a bygone era where she would have fit in perfectly, but a little out of touch with today's world, if you know what I mean."

"So, Paul going off on a rampage like that does sound very much out of character for him," said Chase, jotting down a few notes.

"Oh, absolutely. He's the last person I would have expected to go robbing convenience stores. Though it is true that they were at the end of their rope, with their kid being as sick as he was. At one point, Alice from next door actually organized a meeting of all the neighbors, to ask for money for the Römers, you know. Her idea was to organize a fundraiser so we could get them the funds they needed for the treatment. Honestly, I politely declined. I mean, I'm all for being neighborly and all, but really, giving money so they could fly off to Switzerland to some expensive clinic for some experimental and unproven treatment? I might just as well have set my money on fire. Why couldn't they have selected a clinic right here in the States?"

"So that fundraiser never happened?"

"Alice put something online, but it never reached the threshold to be fully funded, so we all got our money back."

"So you did join the fundraiser?"

She shrugged. "It's very hard to say no when you practically live in each other's pockets. If you don't pay up, they will talk smack behind your back, especially Alice, who's just about the biggest gossipmonger on this whole street. So we put up a token sum of about a hundred bucks, if I recall correctly. But in the end, the whole thing petered out. Though Maria did thank us by baking us a cake, so that was nice."

"When was this? The fundraiser, I mean?"

"Oh, that must have been... six months ago or something? I remember they first got the diagnosis of Hector being sick a year ago, and they went to all the doctors they could find, going from one specialist to the next, but in the end the verdict was that he wasn't going to live, the poor kid. Which is when they started going on about this miracle cure in Switzerland. To be honest, I never believed one word of that. And as I told Rafe, Switzerland is famous for its euthanasia program. So my best guess is they were going to give the kid a shot so he could die with dignity. But then why spend all that money? You can die with dignity anywhere."

For a moment, Odelia seemed to wrestle with her emotions, and I could see why. Raquel Williams wasn't exactly the most kind-hearted person we had met in the course of this investigation, quite the contrary. Finally, she managed to ask, in a sort of strangled voice, "I take it you don't have kids, Mrs. Williams?"

"Raquel, please," she said sweetly. "And no, Rafe and I don't have kids. Not that we couldn't have them, but we didn't want to—a conscious choice. Not a popular one, but the world being as overpopulated as it is, we simply didn't feel it was justified to bring even more people into it. Do you have kids, Mrs. Kingsley?"

"A daughter," said Odelia.

"Oh, isn't that nice," said Raquel.

For a moment, silence reigned as our two detectives seemed to be all out of questions. But finally, Chase took over again, since Odelia seemed incapable of speech. I had the impression there were a few choice words she wanted to say, but those didn't have any bearing on the investigation, so she kept her tongue.

"I know we asked you this last night," said Chase, "but have you had time to think about your statement?" He consulted his notes. "You said you didn't hear anything out of the ordinary, didn't see anything out of the ordinary, and generally have no idea what happened. Is that still a correct representation of your statement, Mrs. Williams?"

"It is," said Raquel immediately. "Though there is one thing I would like to add. You asked me last night if I could think of anyone who would have wanted to harm the Römers, and I said I couldn't think of anyone? Well, I've thought some more, and now I remember that I once witnessed an argument breaking out between Paul Römer and Jim Ward."

"Who's Jim Ward?" asked Odelia.

"He lives across the street," Chase pointed out. "Directly opposite the Römers."

"That's right. He's a real old fuddy-duddy who's impossible to please, really. I once baked him a tray of my famous gingerbread cookies when he was laid up after he'd been run off the road with his bicycle and broke his leg, and he actually threw them in the trash. I know this because I saw them there later. He must have asked his sister, who was living with him while he was convalescing, to throw them out. Which is just a disgrace, really, as I was only trying to help. But anyway, so Paul had planted a tree in his front yard when his son was born. Only there's an unwritten rule that we don't plant trees in our front yards, on account of the fact that it obscures the view, and also, the leaves might fall on the sidewalk and the street and create a mess. It's not a rule set in stone, mind you, but most people in the cul-de-sac prefer not to see any trees planted."

"I didn't know this street was governed by an HOA?" said Chase.

"It isn't. It's an informal thing. All the homeowners get together once or twice a year to discuss things like parking spaces, the possibility of a joint purchase of solar panels to put on our roofs, a very popular initiative, I might add, our summer picnic, the New Year's get-together, the big Christmas tree that we put up in the center of the roundabout, and so on. Mostly it's an opportunity to get together and improve the community spirit. But anyway, so Paul had planted his tree and Jim made it clear that for him, this was absolutely unacceptable. So he told Paul to get rid of the tree, and when Paul demurred, he even went so far as to call the police, who said they couldn't do anything about this tree since it was planted on private property and basically Paul could plant whatever he wanted to."

"Because this association of homeowners isn't actually an HOA."

"Exactly. So Jim could complain until he was blue in the face, that didn't change one thing."

Odelia frowned. "But… there is no tree in the Römer front yard. Is there?"

"No, there is not. Because one night when no one was looking, Jim Ward snuck into Paul's front yard and yanked out that tree by the roots and put it in his wood chipper. Or at least that's what we think happened. Fact is that one morning the tree was gone, and that same morning Jim's wood chipper worked overtime. He claimed that he was doing some work in his backyard, and had nothing to do with any tree disappearing, and that vandals must have taken it, but nobody actually believed him. But since Paul couldn't prove a thing, since the evidence had disappeared, nothing happened."

"And so the tree?"

"Paul thought about planting another one, but finally decided against it. Though I think it was mostly Maria who convinced him not to pursue the matter. She didn't want the aggravation of getting into a big fight over a stupid tree."

"It was important to them, though, since it represented the birth of their son," Odelia pointed out.

"Yeah, symbolically speaking it definitely was important," Raquel agreed. "But instead they planted a new tree in their backyard and a nice flower bed in their front yard, and that made everybody happy."

"And that was the end of the matter?"

"Not exactly," said Raquel with a fine smile. "Paul might have been a really nice guy, but this tree business obviously stung. Which is why one night about a month after the tree incident, someone sprayed weedkiller all over Jim Ward's flower beds, the ones he was so proud of and which had taken him a long time to cultivate. The end result was that both his front and backyard turned into a dead zone. Relations between Jim and the Römers were never the same again."

CHAPTER 10

Fifi hadn't said one word throughout her human's long harangue, but now she piped up, "It's not a bad neighborhood, per se, but there are way too many weirdos living here for my taste. Take that Jim Ward Raquel just mentioned. Now he's probably the biggest weirdo of them all. Every time that man opens his mouth, I cringe. Did you know that he actually managed to lay his hands on a piece of community garden not that far from here? Normally those are only available for people who live in social housing, or don't have access to their own garden. But he got one anyway, through some wrangling, probably because he knows someone on the town council who managed to get his application rubber-stamped."

"But why does he need a community garden when he has his own backyard?" I asked.

"Exactly because of this incident with Paul Römer," said Fifi. "After Paul destroyed his backyard and his front yard with weedkiller, he decided that things weren't safe here for his precious flowers and so he decided to start over again in a different place. A place where Paul wouldn't be able to destroy them again. No one in this neighborhood even knows about this."

"So how do you know?"

"Because I followed him once. I started noticing how he often left home at an ungodly hour, and since he doesn't have a dog, it couldn't be because he had to walk his dog. And since he's retired, he doesn't have to go into the office either. So one morning, I decided to tail him. Which is how I discovered that he spends most of his days in his little patch of greenery."

"Where are these gardens?"

"Out there," she said, pointing due west. "Right next to Farmer Giles's farm, in fact. I believe it used to be a farm, but when the farmer died, it was bought by the town and turned into community gardens for those of us who don't have the luxury of their own backyard. It's pretty neat, too. There must be dozens of little patches of green, and all of them are occupied by avid gardeners, as far as I can tell. Though Jim Ward's patch is the nicest one of them all. He really has a knack for gardening. Which isn't surprising, as he used to be a landscaper."

"Jim Ward is a landscaper?"

"Used to be, before he retired. Which is why it came as such a big blow to him when Paul destroyed his garden, both front and back."

"Allegedly," I said.

"There was nothing alleged about it. I actually saw him do it."

We both stared at the tiny doggie, who was proving a fount of interesting information. "You saw Paul Römer destroy Jim Ward's garden?"

"I did. It was the middle of the night, and I woke up from a strange rustling sound, so I decided to investigate. I popped out of the pet flap and looked for the source of the sound. The rustling I'd heard wasn't actually rustling but the spraying sound of the nozzle on the weedkiller Paul used. He had a balaclava pulled over his head and was dressed in black, but I still recognized him easily. At first, I wondered what he was doing, but then it became clear to me he was using some powerful toxin and spraying it all over Jim's lovely flower beds. When he was done at the front of the house, he snuck around the back and continued his dirty work. When all was said and done, everything was dead, and Jim's gorgeous flower beds were a devastated area. He'd actually entered the annual flower show, you know, which was to be held the next weekend, so his flowers looked extra beautiful, and he'd taken great care to make his gardens stand out. And he might have pulled it off and won the big prize, but after Paul's intervention, he had to pull out of the show. I don't think I've ever seen a man look as crestfallen as Jim did when he surveyed the damage. As if someone had taken a dagger and stabbed him straight through the heart."

"Poor man," said Dooley. "That wasn't very nice of Paul, was it, Max?"

"No, but it also wasn't very nice of Jim to destroy Paul's tree."

"Yeah, he probably shouldn't have done that," Fifi agreed. "It set off a chain of events that could have been prevented if they had all treated each other with a little more civility."

"How did Jim retaliate?" I asked.

"He didn't. Not as far as I know. He took that patch in the community gardens the town provided and kept it a secret, but I don't think he actually took revenge on Paul."

"Unless it was Jim who murdered Paul and his family last night," I pointed out.

"I very much doubt it," said Fifi. "Jim might be capable of killing trees, but I don't think he's in the business of killing human beings. It takes a very special type of person to do that kind of thing, and Jim is essentially a kind man."

"Raquel doesn't seem to like him very much."

"That's because Raquel doesn't like anyone," said Fifi. "Except me, of course."

"And Rafe."

Fifi made a face. "Maybe. The jury is still out on that one." We laughed at this. "At least she loves you," said Dooley.

"Yeah, she does. Sometimes I think she only loves me. Some people are incapable of loving other people, you know, and transfer their affections to their dogs. Or maybe to their cats," she added on a doubtful note.

OUR NEXT PORT of call was Jim Ward himself, and as luck would have it, we found the retired landscaper home. I'd told Odelia about what Fifi had revealed to us, and she was glad we had gleaned the information.

Mr. Ward didn't look particularly pleased to see us, but then that could probably be said about a lot of people, as I've already indicated. "Is this about the Römers again?" he asked when he opened the door. "I told that cop last night everything I have to say, which is that I don't know anything." He was a gray-haired old man with a stoop and bristling eyebrows he might do best to put his garden shears to if I had a say in the matter.

"We just wanted to ask you a few more questions if that's all right with you, Mr. Ward," said Odelia.

It clearly wasn't all right with the man, but since we didn't offer him a choice, he reluctantly allowed us to enter his little home. I took a closer look at his front yard and saw that it was devoid of flowers of any description and consisted solely of grass and a single hardy shrub planted in the middle. I wondered if his backyard was the same way. It didn't take us long to find out, for as he led us into the living room, I immediately glanced out his back window and saw that his backyard was all grass, with a hedge bordering it on all sides. Easy to maintain, but definitely not very ambitious for a retired landscaper.

"So, what do you want to know?" he asked, and I noticed that this man didn't offer us any chocolate chip cookies or even coffee or tea. He simply wanted to get rid of us as fast as he could.

"It has come to our attention that you and Paul Römer got involved in a dispute over a tree Paul had planted in his front yard," said Chase, opening the proceedings with a shot across the bow.

Mr. Ward's bushy brows worked furiously. "Who told you that?" But when Chase stayed mum, he grumbled, "That's all ancient history. Happened years and years ago."

"Not that long ago," Chase said. "Paul and Maria's son Hector was six when he died, and Paul planted that tree when Hector was born."

"You don't have to tell me. I was there. I lived it," the man grunted. He pulled out a chair from underneath the dining room table but didn't offer Odelia and Chase seats, so they were forced to remain standing. "Look, we had an agreement: no trees planted in our front yards," he said with the air of a man who is forced to dredge up an old story he's been forced to tell a million times. "And Paul Römer knew that perfectly well when he bought the house. No trees. So when he decided to go against the collective wisdom of the entire neighborhood, he should have known that it wouldn't go down well. The others all caved, not wanting to get into an argument, so I decided to step up. I went over there and told him point-blank that he should remove that tree and plant it out back instead. He refused. He said he used to have a similar tree in his childhood home, planted when he was a kid, and he loved the idea of Hector growing up and watching that tree from his bedroom window. So I told him to switch rooms so Hector could have his room at the back where he could look into the backyard instead. But Paul insisted. He said it wasn't the same thing, and that there was something about a nice tree growing in front of your house that appealed to him. Which I understood, of course. But not here. Not in this neighborhood."

"And so you yanked out that tree and fed it to your wood chipper," said Chase.

Jim's face remained impassive. "I did not do that," he insisted.

"Paul Römer believed you did, which is why a couple of weeks after the incident, he doused your flower beds with weedkiller and turned your beautiful garden into a devastated area."

His face sagged. "That, I believe," he said. "Which is why my garden still looks like this." He gestured to the green lawn out back, smooth as a pool table.

"Surely by now the effects of that weedkiller must be gone," said Odelia. "So you can plant flowers again?"

"As long as Paul was alive, I didn't want to take the chance," said Jim. Then he seemed to realize what he was saying and quickly backtracked. "I mean, I didn't trust the man after what he did, so I didn't want to give him the opportunity to repeat the procedure."

"Which is why you applied for and were granted permission to cultivate a piece of community garden next to Farmer Giles's field," said Odelia.

This time his jaw actually dropped. "How do you..." But then he realized who he was talking to. "Of course. You're cops. You would know about these things." He dragged a hand through his bristly white hair. "Look, I know I'm probably not entitled to a piece of land out there, but after what

Paul did, I simply had no other choice. Gardening is my life. Take that away from me, like Paul did, and you destroy my soul. So I had to find a solution. And I've been happily tending to my little patch of paradise for five years now. They even asked me to take on the role of supervisor, but I've been holding off on that. I don't want to lord it over other people. All I want is to be able to potter about my little patch in peace."

"So even after all these years, you clearly still hadn't forgiven Paul," said Chase.

The man tapped the table while he thought how to answer that one. "No," he said finally. "I don't think I had. When he destroyed my gardens—plural—I had just entered the annual flower competition. And it wasn't just that I had to pull out at the last minute, but those gardens were my life's work. I'd spent every possible minute in them and poured my heart and soul into turning them into something absolutely beautiful. And so when he destroyed them, it felt as if he'd stepped on my soul and yanked my heart straight out of my chest."

"You were angry."

"I was, yeah. Wouldn't you be?"

"And so you waited five years until the perfect moment and killed him."

His eyes went wide, and he actually got up from behind the table. "No!"

"And because you didn't want to leave any witnesses, you also killed his wife and his son, the one this all started with when Paul planted a tree in his honor."

"No, I didn't! Okay, so I hated Paul Römer for what he did to me, but I didn't kill the guy. I would never..." He had to steady himself against the table, and Odelia stepped forward to lend him a helping hand and sit him down again. For a moment, we all feared that the man would keel over, but finally his breathing slowed again, and he repeated, "I did not kill Paul Römer. You have to believe me. I would never do such a terrible thing. Though it is true that I got my own revenge on the Römers."

"How?" asked Chase curtly.

The man swallowed. "Maria was extremely fond of the chocolate chip cookies she made. So much so that she trotted them out every year at our summer picnic. She said it was a special recipe handed down through the generations from mother to daughter. And they were excellent, no doubt about it. I noticed how Raquel was jealous of Maria, not just about the cookies, but in general. Maria was an exceptional woman. Unlike Raquel, she was a natural beauty, but she was also beautiful inside, you know. She was simply a wonderful person, inside and out, with a kind heart and a sweet disposition. But for some reason, Raquel simply couldn't stand her. Once, during one of these picnics, I decided to sneak into the Römer place when no one was looking and steal Maria's chocolate chip cookie recipe and give it to Raquel. So the next time the Williamses invited the Römers over for dinner, Raquel had made those very same cookies and offered them as dessert. According to what Raquel later told me, Maria was so shocked she actually had to leave. Her precious secret recipe had been stolen by Raquel." He sighed deeply. "I felt deeply troubled afterward, since it wasn't Maria I wanted to suffer but Paul. But what was done was done, and Raquel never stopped showcasing 'her' cookies after that, and Maria stopped baking them."

"Yeah, we tasted them just now," said Odelia. "They're delicious."

"They are," Jim confirmed. He eyed the detectives anxiously. "But you have to believe me, detectives. I didn't murder the Römers. I simply couldn't do something like that."

"Did Paul or Maria ever mention anything to you about this animosity between themselves and the Williamses?" asked Chase.

Jim shook his head. "I wasn't on speaking terms with the Römers, as you can probably imagine. At first, Maria tried to play go-between between me and her husband, but clearly Paul wouldn't have it, and frankly, I wasn't interested in making amends either. He'd gone too far for that."

"You did destroy the tree he planted for his kid," Chase pointed out.

Jim hesitated, then finally nodded. "Okay, I'll admit to that. I did pull out that tree and put it through my wood chipper. And in hindsight, maybe I shouldn't have done it. I could have spared myself a lot of misery if I hadn't. But rules are rules, and I was incensed when Paul decided to trample all over them." He paused.

"Yes?" said Odelia.

"It's probably not important," said Jim. "And it's got nothing to do with what happened to the Römers, but now that you're here I might as well tell you since it's been on my mind. Early this morning I saw a strange figure over by the community gardens. A hooded figure I didn't recognize, and I've been there long enough to know everyone down there."

"Maybe a newcomer?" Chase suggested.

"I thought the same thing at first, but there are no newcomers. It's all old-timers like me. Young people don't seem to have a big interest in gardening, so we've been the same small crowd for years now. And this figure seemed to know his way around there, too, which is what attracted my attention in the first place." He shrugged. "Just thought you'd want to know."

"Thanks, Mr. Ward."

"You think this person was a man?" asked Odelia.

"I do, from the way he moved. Though I never saw his

face, so I couldn't be sure." He tapped the table with his fingers. "And then there's something else... my neighbor didn't turn up this morning. Bill Taylor. He tends to the patch next to mine. Now it's probably nothing, but he's usually out there even before I arrive, and this morning he wasn't there."

"Maybe he's ill," Odelia suggested.

"It's certainly possible," said Jim. "Though if he was, I would probably have heard about it, or one of the others would have, since we like to stay in touch. Anyway, I'm sure there's a perfectly reasonable explanation. And tomorrow morning he'll show up and he'll tell me all about it."

CHAPTER 11

Our next port of call was Dolores Peltz. We found the dispatcher at home, enjoying a rare vacation day. Though when she opened the door, I could tell she had been crying, and so maybe her day off wasn't so much a vacation as a day of mourning for her good friend Maria Römer.

"So, you've heard?" said Chase. Dolores nodded wordlessly, and he gave her a heartfelt hug, and then Odelia did the same. She sighed and invited us into the house, which was a cozy little place that appealed to me immediately. It was located in a quiet neighborhood, and when I glanced out the back, I was struck by a riot of color in the form of flowers of many descriptions and variety. All in all, it looked as if Dolores had as much of a green thumb as Jim Ward did.

Dolores and her two colleagues had taken a seat in her salon, and she wiped her eyes with a napkin. "Alec told me personally. He came out here and told me that Maria died last night, apparently killed by Paul, which I find very hard to believe, to be honest. Then again, it's always possible, of course. In our line of work, we know that people are probably capable of anything, so I wouldn't put it past him, but still..." She was quiet for a moment. "They were such a devoted couple, you know. And Paul loved that little boy of his to death." She shook her head. "I mean..."

"Yeah, we know what you mean," Chase assured her. "So you never saw any signs of trouble in their marriage? Fights over money or anything?"

"Nothing," said Dolores. "Which is why this came as such a big shock to all of us who knew them well. Maria was just such a wonderful person. She was such a gentle soul. When she first started working at the station, I didn't think I'd end up being such good friends with her because we were both so different. She was soft-spoken, sweet-natured, and always had a kind word to say to everyone, while I'm... well, let's just say I'm the exact opposite. But somehow we became friends, and even after she got pregnant and decided to stop working and stay home to look after Hector, we remained friends. We didn't see each other all the time, but we met up occasionally."

"When was the last time you saw her?" asked Chase.

"Um... a couple of months ago. We met up for drinks and then went shopping together."

"Did she mention anything about Hector's illness?"

"She did, yeah. She said they found a great clinic and they were going to try and get Hector in there. It was very expensive, though, and she said they were thinking about selling the house. But they already had two mortgages, so I didn't think that would be enough, so I suggested asking the colleagues to collect money for Hector. But she said her next-door neighbor had set up a fundraiser online, and she hoped it would net them enough to send Hector to this clinic. But then apparently things didn't work out exactly as she'd hoped. She told me over the phone after the event."

"Yeah, that fundraiser didn't happen," said Odelia. "Any idea why?"

"According to what Maria told me, it was sabotaged by another one of her neighbors."

"Sabotaged? By whom?"

"Um… I think she mentioned the name Raquel. It was just a suspicion she had. She wasn't sure. But apparently, the fundraiser was going really great, with people asking their friends and family to chip in, and they were getting a lot of traction. But then, suddenly, it simply stalled, and they didn't manage to reach their target on time, so everyone who donated got their money back."

"But how can you sabotage a fundraiser?" asked Odelia.

"From what Maria told me, a rumor was being spread online, on social media, that Hector wasn't sick at all, and that the fundraiser was just a way to collect enough funds so the Römers could take an expensive vacation in Europe. They couldn't afford it, so they made up this sob story about Hector being sick. Maria sent me a link to the post, and it had this picture of Hector looking absolutely happy and healthy. It got a lot of likes and shares and the post quickly went viral."

"And Raquel posted this?" asked Odelia, looking utterly shocked.

"Not under her own name, obviously. She used a dummy account. But Maria was pretty sure Raquel must have been behind it since she couldn't think of anyone else who would do such a terrible thing. From what she told me, Raquel had some kind of animosity against Maria for some mysterious reason. Maria told me this crazy story about Raquel once stealing her cookies so she could sell them. And also of her stealing her family recipe and feeding them her own cookies."

"Yeah, we heard that story," said Odelia. "Though we hadn't heard about what happened with the fundraiser.

Though from talking to Raquel just now, I can certainly believe she would be capable of such a horrible thing."

"Illegal, also," Dolores pointed out. "If sabotaging that fundraiser would have led to Hector's death, I'm sure the Römers could have brought charges."

"They first would have had to prove Raquel's involvement," said Chase.

"That's easy. A lawyer can subpoena Facebook and demand they produce the IP address of the person posting those messages. Raquel may think she's clever, but she probably isn't clever enough to hide her IP address." She wiped a tear from her eyes. "And now Paul has gone and killed his family. It's such a tragedy. And totally avoidable. If only they'd managed to raise those funds."

"So you think Paul killed his wife and kid because he was desperate?"

"Why else? If he thought his son was going to die within the next couple of months and there was nothing he could do to stop it..." She shook her head. "I just wish she'd talked to me, you know. I could have done something. I could have talked to you," she told Odelia. "The thought had occurred to me that you could write an article and maybe try to raise funds that way. But Maria told me that she had everything under control and that a solution was imminent."

"Paul robbed a dozen convenience stores and gas stations last night," Chase pointed out. "So maybe that was the solution Maria was referring to?"

"Oh, God," said Dolores, burying her face in her hands.

"The money has disappeared, though," said Chase. "So he probably hid it before he returned home. You wouldn't know where he could have hidden it, do you?"

Dolores shook her head. "No idea. Though I doubt whether he'd have been able to get the necessary funds together."

"Why? How much was this treatment going to cost?"

"Several hundred thousand," said Dolores.

"That's a lot of money."

"It is a lot. But if that fundraiser hadn't been sabotaged, you'd be surprised how much a dedicated community can raise. I'm sure they would have managed in the end."

"I talked to several of the owners of these convenience stores," said Chase, "and asked them to give me a ballpark number of the amount Paul stole."

"And? How much?"

"Twenty thousand, maybe? Definitely not the number you're mentioning."

"Yeah, if that was Maria and Paul's big solution, it wasn't going to cut it."

"Which is probably what Paul realized as he counted his haul before he got home," said Chase. "That it wasn't going to be enough. And that he'd just blown his last chance, since the police would be on his doorstep in a matter of hours."

They were all quiet for a moment as they thought about those final hours in the lives of Paul and Maria Römer and their beloved boy, and even Dooley and I didn't say a word as we wondered about what could have been.

CHAPTER 12

It wasn't hard to see why Maria would have thought that her neighbor Raquel sabotaged that vital fundraiser on which the Römers had pinned their hopes. If Maria knew about the cookie debacle, she would have figured that if Raquel was capable of stealing her precious family recipe, she was also capable of spreading vile gossip about her on social media. But there was one other person in the cul-de-sac who had it in for the Römers, and that was Jim Ward, whose beloved flowers had been destroyed by Paul. And so it could also have been Jim who had destroyed the Römers' chance to collect enough money to send Hector to Switzerland for this treatment.

As we were in the car traveling back to the cul-de-sac for another interview with Raquel, Dooley and I discussed the case, and we both agreed that Jim Ward clearly had the biggest motive to cause the Römers harm. But would he resort to murder?

"I think," said Dooley, "that Paul murdered his family because he felt pushed with his back up against the wall. And possibly Maria and Paul decided this together. But the person responsible is the one who sabotaged that fundraiser and took away their chance to save their boy. They didn't hold the gun or pull the trigger, but in my opinion, they're just as guilty of murder as Paul is."

"You're absolutely right," I said. "Though in the eyes of the law, that probably doesn't constitute murder, Dooley." Though if they could prove that Raquel was behind that sabotage, they probably could bring charges against her, I thought.

"It should be," said Dooley with a touch of forcefulness he usually didn't display. "It's a terrible thing that woman did, Max, and she should suffer the consequences."

"I know," I said. And I had the impression that both Odelia and Chase felt the same way, since we were now on our way to pick up Raquel, and this time they were going to interview her over at the police station and not in her lovely home with the smell of chocolate chip cookies in the air.

It didn't take us long to return to the cul-de-sac, and to say that Raquel was surprised to see us again would be an understatement. Though when Chase arrested her on the spot and escorted her to the car, she was even more surprised. All across the cul-de-sac, neighbors actually stepped out of their houses and watched the proceedings with a curious eye, and I wondered how they would have known about the impending arrest. Apparently, they possessed some kind of sixth sense for these sorts of things.

Twenty minutes later, Raquel was seated in interview room number one, with Chase sitting across from her. Of her former chipper demeanor, there was not a single trace left, and she suddenly looked about a decade older.

"But I didn't sabotage that fundraiser!" she cried. "I didn't! I would never do such a thing—never!"

"But you did tell us that you didn't think it was fair for the Römers to collect money for the treatment of their kid, and that you felt forced to put in a token amount because otherwise the neighbors would point the finger at you."

"Well, yeah, of course, I said that because it's true. If you don't follow the rules, you get punished. Just look at what happened with Paul and his tree. He thought he was doing a good thing for his boy, and it set off this crazy feud that led to Jim destroying his tree, then Paul destroying Jim's flowers, and Jim retaliating by stealing Maria's recipe and handing it to me so I could shove her precious cookies in her face."

"So you admit that you stole Maria's recipe?"

"I didn't steal her recipe, Jim did, and then handed it to me. And I probably shouldn't have passed the recipe off as my own. That was wrong of me. But then I simply couldn't stand Maria's holier-than-thou attitude, as if she was the only honorable person on the planet, and the rest of us were simple sinners. I just wanted to wipe that annoying smirk off her face, and I succeeded."

"You also told us that you think there are already too many kids being born, and the world is overpopulated as it is. And you also mentioned how they should have used the money from that fundraiser for euthanasia, so maybe Hector Römer dying would be a good thing?"

"I never said that! Now you're twisting my words! All I said was that overpopulation is real, and that's why Rafe and I decided not to have kids. And that part about euthanasia... I probably shouldn't have said that. And I didn't really mean it either. Hector was a sweet kid, and he didn't deserve to die."

"Did you really decide not to have children, Raquel?" Chase pressed. "Or was the decision forced upon you and your husband?"

She wavered a moment, then finally relented, "Okay, so I can't have kids. But that has nothing to do with anything."

"You couldn't have kids, and you lived next door to a couple who had a kid and were clearly happy and living the kind of life you and your husband could only dream of. So frankly speaking, I wouldn't be surprised if you decided to put them down a peg by sabotaging that fundraiser when you had the chance."

"No!" she practically screamed, and I thought she was very convincing. She may have stolen Maria's cookies, but I didn't have the impression she would have gone to these lengths to sabotage her neighbors' happiness.

"So if you didn't do it, who did?" asked Chase. "And remember we can always subpoena Facebook and find out who was behind that campaign."

"I don't know," she said, sinking back down in her seat. "Jim, maybe? Though he's probably too old for that kind of thing. I don't even think he has a computer, much less a Facebook account."

"Could your husband be behind this?"

She shook her head. "He thought stealing those cookies was a bad idea, and after I baked them and offered them to the Römers, he was so mad with me. He said this kind of petty behavior was ruining our relationship with all of our neighbors, and it simply wasn't worth it. He believes in adopting a live-and-let-live attitude when it comes to this sort of thing." She blinked at the detective. "So... are you going to lock me up in jail now? For stealing those cookies?"

Chase grimaced. "It's not the cookies, Raquel. You can see that, right?"

"But I didn't post nasty things about Hector," she said quietly. "I didn't."

In the end, Chase decided to let her go. He had sent a request to Facebook to release the information, and if that didn't work a subpoena would follow, so now we had to wait for what they would come back with. As it was, he wasn't fully convinced Raquel was the one behind the campaign, and neither was Odelia, even though she clearly wasn't

Raquel's biggest fan after the things she had said about euthanasia and the fundraiser being a waste of money and time.

Chase considered picking up Raquel's husband but preferred to wait for the data to come in about the social media campaign targeting Hector Römer. If the Williamses were behind it, the information would bear it out, and they could always make the arrests later. Though according to Uncle Alec, there wasn't a whole lot they could bring against them in the way of charges. Defamation of character was punishable by law, but to link that to the death of the Römers was going to be very hard to prove in a court of law. Still, Chase said he was going to give it his best shot, and we could only admire him for it.

CHAPTER 13

Jim Ward was back at his beloved little patch of heaven tending to his hydrangeas when a sudden urge came over him to dig a little deeper into the mystery of his missing neighbor. He had told those cops who had paid him a visit about the affair, and also about the mysterious person he'd seen traipsing about yesterday, but he was pretty sure that they weren't interested in pursuing the matter any further. He'd given a lot of thought to that interview and had been playing it over in his mind several times, going over what he had said and what they had said, and eventually, he thought he probably had told them too much. Like admitting to the fact that he had destroyed Paul's tree. They could still bring charges against him for that. Criminal damage, maybe. That could cost him a pretty penny. Worse if he had to get a lawyer, and even worse if Paul's relatives or Maria's decided to sue him after the fact. Stranger things had happened.

But then these cops were good, he had to admit. He had told them things he never intended to tell anyone. And how had they found out so soon that he had a piece of the community gardens? As far as he could tell, he'd never told that to anyone. They must have done some background checking on him and the other neighbors. But to what end he didn't understand. Obviously, the whole thing was a terrible tragedy, but then people often engaged in such behavior. You read stories in the paper almost every single day about people murdering their entire families for this reason or that, and nobody was to blame except those people themselves. As far as he knew, the police never went around looking for a neighbor they could pin the blame on. If they did that, they could probably find a lot of so-called suspects. Maybe Paul's boss hadn't been nice to him the day before, or someone had cut him off in traffic on his way home, or an unhappy client at the bank had shouted at him. Would they also interview those people? Blame them for what Paul had done?

He now glanced around himself and downed tools for a moment and wiped his hands on his blue coveralls, then got up as quickly as his aged knees allowed from the foam kneeling pad he liked to use and snuck over to the little gate that only reached until his waist and divided his garden from the next, which belonged to Bill Taylor. Every plot also had a small garden house where the gardeners kept their gear. He kept his locked at all times, since there had been a spate of break-ins and he kept all of his tools in there, most of them dating back to his working days as a landscaper, and some of them were quite valuable and frankly irreplaceable as far as he was concerned.

He looked around himself to make sure he wasn't being observed, then stepped over the little gate and walked up the stone path to the garden house belonging to his neighbor. He then saw that Bill hadn't locked it, with the hasp unsecured by the padlock. He opened the garden house and was immediately shocked by the powerful smell that assaulted his nostrils. It almost smelled as if something had died in there. A rat, maybe, or some other rodent. But the moment his eyes had adjusted to the darkness, he saw it wasn't a rat that caused the terrible smell. Seated on top of his cordless lawnmower was the body of Bill Taylor, and the man was obviously dead.

* * *

JUST WHEN I thought it was probably time to head to Odelia's office and enjoy a nice long nap until dinnertime, a call came in and Chase, who took it, looked grim. We were in the man's office, with Chase and Odelia discussing the ins and outs of the case they had decided to tackle. He put down the phone and said, "Remember the story Jim Ward told us about his neighbor not showing up at the community gardens this morning? He found him in his garden house. Dead."

"Murdered?" asked Odelia immediately, indicating that she had murder on her mind.

"Stabbed to death. So I think it's probably best if we go over there and take a closer look."

And so it was that Dooley and I found ourselves back in Chase's squad car, on the road to another crime scene.

The community gardens had been a project instigated by one of our previous mayors, as a way to offer those people who didn't own a house and therefore had no access to a garden, a way to practice their gardening skills and also their community spirit. Mostly these plots of land were tended to by people who liked to grow their own veggies, for when we arrived there I saw many tomato plants, cucumber, squashes, peppers, beans, eggplant, but also so-called herb spirals that were all the rage. Some people preferred flowers, of course, and had turned their beloved gardens into small patches of delight, with a chair and a table where they could sit and enjoy the fruits of their labor. Jim Ward's garden was a mix of both. He had his hydrangeas but he also had his tomato plants and a herbaceous border. Next to him was a garden that looked equally lovely, carefully tended to by a green thumb or two. And since we'd had a lot of rain lately, this garden was an absolute riot of color. This had been William —or Bill—Taylor's part of the gardens.

Crime scene people had already arrived, and also several police officers to guard the scene and interview witnesses, of which there were many, since after all the rain the sun had come out and people arrived in droves. Though they could also have been attracted by the news that a body had been found. Nothing guarantees a good crowd like a dead body found in a community garden.

Jim was being interviewed by a young police officer, and the man looked decidedly stricken, so I assumed that Mr. Taylor must have been a good friend, not a mere neighbor.

I would have inspected the garden house where the man's body was found, but frankly, I was running on fumes since I hadn't eaten, and I didn't think my stomach would take kindly to witnessing such a disturbing scene. So Dooley and I both decided to stay away and let Odelia and Chase do the looking and report back to us the particulars of this affair. Mostly I was interested to know if Bill Taylor was murdered or if he had died by his own hand, which was entirely possible, as he was an avid gardener, and possibly his begonias hadn't come out the way he'd anticipated.

It didn't take long for Odelia to return, and as we sought and found a quiet place where we wouldn't be overheard, I noticed she was looking a little green around the gills, indicating it must have been quite the sight in that little garden house. Her next words confirmed this suspicion.

"According to Abe Cornwall, he sustained a knife wound to the abdomen and bled to death."

"So it was murder," I said.

"Unless he stabbed himself in the belly, then yeah. And since no knife was found, the theory of the self-inflicted wound seems highly unlikely."

"Who in their right mind would murder a gardener?" I asked.

"Looks like we've got another case on our hands," said Odelia as she chewed her lip. "As if we didn't have enough to contend with already."

"Who was this Bill Taylor?" asked Dooley.

"Well, that's the interesting part," said Odelia. "We don't know. My uncle's officers have already talked to several of the people here, and none of them really knew him. Even Jim said he didn't know the man all that well. All he knew was that he was from Boston originally and was a retired businessman. Apparently, he was the type of person who liked to keep himself to himself and revealed very little about his background. According to Abe he was probably in his early seventies when he died, but so far that's it. But don't worry. We'll find out soon enough."

Abe Cornwall is our county coroner and has probably seen every possible murder scene possible. So if he said Bill Taylor was in his seventies, there was no doubt that he was. And if he said it was murder, we were faced with another murder case to solve. Though to be honest, the Römer case seemed to have petered out a little since it had pretty much been decided that it was murder-suicide and that Paul Römer was the man who had handled the gun. And since the other case on Chase's plate, the Turner double homicide, had also been put to bed with Mark Turner as the obvious culprit, we could now focus on Mr. Taylor and who had ended the poor man's life.

"At least he died surrounded by his beloved plants," said Dooley, always eager to provide the positive note.

Odelia smiled. "Yeah, at least there's that." She then asked us to hunt around for clues, if we could find them, in the way of pet witnesses, while she returned to assist Chase in this new investigation.

Moments later, Dooley and I were roaming around these community gardens, admiring the view, and generally hoping to run into a pet of any description we could talk to regarding this baffling murder of the amateur gardener. Contrary to what we had hoped, after talking to two poodles who were there with their owners and also a lone black cat who just happened to pass by, we found that none of them could enlighten us in regards to the murder that had taken place. So we took a breather and watched the scene as officers interviewed everyone and all, and Chase and Odelia discussed the case with Abe Cornwall. The paunchy coroner seemed a little nervous, so I figured he probably had a backlog of bodies he needed to get processed down at the morgue. It often happens that the man is overworked and the coroner's office buzzing at full tilt. And then at other times, there seems to be a sudden dearth of suspicious deaths. All part of the business of being a coroner, I guess, or is the correct term medical examiner? I can never tell these two apart.

And we'd sat there for a few minutes, feeling a little useless, to be honest, when suddenly a butterfly landed on a nearby flower and addressed me. "Say, you're Max, aren't you?"

"That's right," I said. "Who's asking?"

"My name is also Max," said the butterfly. "You're that detective, is that correct?"

"I am a cat detective," I confirmed, surprised that my reputation would have spread to the bug kingdom. Though it was true that we had been in communication with butterflies in the past, and even flies, if I remembered correctly.

"Great," said the butterfly. "Then maybe you can tell me when they're going to remove the body of that dead guy from that shed over there. It's just that it stinks up the place, you know, and it's not a lot of fun for us."

"I didn't know a dead body could be so annoying to a butterfly's sense of smell?" I said, much surprised by this confession.

"Well, it is. We have very sensitive antennae, and dead bodies don't agree with us very much. Flies, sure. Maggots, oh, they're probably having a ball right now, feeding on this fella. But us butterflies prefer a more subtle bouquet if you catch my drift."

"Flowers and such," I said, nodding.

"You got it, Max." He glanced over at Dooley. "And you're Max's famous sidekick Dooley, aren't you?"

"That's correct," said Dooley proudly. "I like to assist Max in his investigations, and for what it's worth, he always gets his man, even if it's a woman."

"He's like the Canadian Mounties, then," the butterfly quipped.

"Something like that," I allowed with a smile. "So did you know the dead man?"

"Oh, I've seen him around," said the butterfly. "Pottering about in his garden, you know. Though I prefer that guy over there, if I'm honest."

"Who, Jim Ward?"

"That's the one. He loves flowers almost as much as we do. And he plants them to our heart's content. Though you should tell him not to bother with the tomatoes, it's not gonna work. This soil isn't conducive to tomatoes."

"I'll be sure to tell him," I promised. "So about Bill Taylor…"

"Who?"

"The dead man."

"Oh, right." He grinned at me. "I know the drill, Max. Now you're gonna ask me about fingerprints and footprints and cigarette butts and all of that jazz. But to be perfectly honest with you, I don't know anything about that. What I do know is who made him so."

We both stared at the butterfly. "What do you mean?" I asked finally, wondering if it could be so. If Max had actually witnessed the murder.

"The guy who killed him, I mean. I saw him, you know."

"You witnessed the murder?" I asked, excitement making me a little lightheaded all of a sudden.

"I did! I was taking a breather on the shed's window ledge when I saw two guys getting into some kind of argument. And then one of the guys suddenly took out a knife and stuck it into the other guy. And then, probably because he wasn't sure he got it right the first time, he repeated the procedure. The other guy sort of slumped, and I figured the treatment wasn't doing him a lot of good. But then the killer dropped the knife and left, and the other guy keeled over and expired. At least I think he did, since I didn't actually go in there and feel for a pulse or anything."

"And so the killer, what did he look like?"

"Beats me. He was wearing one of those hoodies that are all the rage. And the annoying thing about those hoodies is that they hide a person's face, though that's probably the whole idea."

"But you're certain it was a man and not a woman?"

"Positive. He was a big fella, big and hulking. And he moved like a dude, you know." And he proceeded to give us a full description of the killer's outfit, complete with baggy pants, sneakers, and the hoodie in question. It wasn't much, but it was definitely something. And the thing that stood out the most was that the killer's sneakers had been a vivid orange, which might bode well for the investigation. How many large men walked around with bright orange sneakers? Possibly not all that many.

And so we profusely thanked the butterfly for his contribution, and then hastened to Odelia's side, giving her the sign that we had some information to share with her. She followed us to that same secluded spot behind a nearby garden house, and we proceeded to pour the witness statement of the butterfly into her ear. As expected, she was over the moon, since apparently no one else had so far come forward to give them evidence that might lead to the identification and subsequent arrest of Mr. Taylor's killer, so we'd pulled off quite a coup.

She promised to tell Chase and to be on the lookout for a man answering to the killer's description, which sounded a lot like the mystery man Jim had seen, and I had a feeling it wouldn't be long before this person was captured and the motives for his crime revealed.

CHAPTER 14

Chase had decided to look a little deeper into the possible connection between the murder of Bill Taylor and the hoodlums that had been terrorizing the cul-de-sac where the Römers had lived. After all, the community garden wasn't all that far removed from that cul-de-sac. As the crow flies probably no more than a couple of hundred yards, all in all. If you started from the backyard of the Römer house and traversed the fields, you could reach those gardens in a couple of minutes on foot, which is what Jim Ward did on a daily basis.

Was it possible that one of those hooligans, as Jim had called them, had followed him one day and then returned later on, mistaking Bill Taylor for Jim and deciding to pay him back for some perceived slight? The relationship between the neighborhood and those kids had always been bad and had worsened a lot after they had attacked Mrs. Flower, who had ended up in the hospital and was still there according to the last reports.

Chase had put it to Jim straight: did you ever get into an argument with those kids? And of course, Jim being Jim, he had confessed that he did. Once when he passed them in his car, he swerved off the road, jumped the curb, and almost hit one of them. Instead of hitting the kid, he had hit one of their bikes, probably reducing it to the scrapheap. They had raced after him, shouting a lot of verbal abuse at him, but he had managed to get away clean, feeling satisfied that he'd avenged the attack on his good friend Mrs. Flower.

"But weren't you afraid of their reprisal?" asked Chase.

"Of course! But it was one of those spur-of-the-moment things, you know. Those kids were there, gathered on the sidewalk hanging out, and all I could think of was Angie Flower, her face as white as the sheet of the hospital bed she was lying in, and I suddenly felt so angry I couldn't think straight. I would have wiped them all from the sidewalk if I could, but common sense returned, and I changed my mind. But not before I managed to demolish one of their bikes."

"You shouldn't do these things, Mr. Ward," said Chase. "It's dangerous, not to mention illegal, to take the law into your own hands."

"Then you better get those kids off the street and out of our neighborhood because if this goes on much longer, there will be more trouble, I can promise you that." He gulped a little. "And their next victim just might be me."

Which is what had given Chase the idea that they may have already tried to avenge the destruction of their motorcycle by murdering Bill Taylor, mistaking him for Mr. Ward. In which case, they could narrow their investigation to these kids. The problem was that they had stopped hanging out there the moment the investigation into the deaths of the Römer family had started and hadn't been back. They probably didn't enjoy the massive police presence and had decided to look for a different place to hang out.

But something told us that they would be back. Once the police presence was gone, and the neighborhood was quiet again, they'd probably return. And since Chase was the kind of person who liked to have a plan, by the time we got home that night, he had already formed one and told us all about it over dinner.

I was glad for the respite, since it had been a busy night and day, and I could really use a nice prolonged nap and a bite to eat. But when we arrived home, I discovered to my dismay that my spot on the couch had been taken... by Mooch! Now, I like Mooch. It may even be said that I thought he was a great dog and deserved to be treated with all the respect that we could muster. After the ordeal he'd gone through, it was the least we could do. But I drew the line at taking my spot on the couch. Okay, so the couch is probably big enough to accommodate more than one pet, you say? That's true, but I have my designated spot, and I don't like it when other pets squat on my piece of preferred real estate. But since I'm essentially a kind-hearted cat, I decided not to say anything and allow Mooch to remain there for now. He probably wouldn't be staying with us long, so as soon as he was gone, I'd have my spot back. But in spite of this, I still couldn't help but glare at him to some extent as I took up position on the opposite side of the couch.

From time to time, he opened his eyes and gave me a curious look, but then closed them again. Finally, I guess he couldn't take it anymore, and he asked, "Is it something I said, Max?"

"Oh, no, absolutely not," I assured him. "Just tired, you know. It's been a long day."

He closed his eyes again, then opened them. "It's just that... you seem upset with me for some reason."

"I'm not upset," I assured him. "Just tired, like I said."

"Okay, if you say so." For a moment, neither one of us spoke, but then Dooley, who had jumped up on the couch next to Mooch, stared at the bulldog. "Why are you in Max's spot, Mooch?"

Mooch looked slightly perturbed. "Max's spot? I didn't know this was Max's spot."

"Well, it is. We all have our designated spots on the couch, and you're in Max's."

"Oh, I'm sorry," said Mooch, and he looked so crestfallen that I felt guilty.

"Please stay where you are," I said. "My spot is your spot, after all."

"Are you sure?" he asked.

"Absolutely," I said magnanimously. "Please be my guest."

"Thanks, Max. That's so kind of you, you know. In fact, I didn't even know that cats could be as kind as you guys have been. Of all the cats I've known, you guys must by far be the nicest ones."

"Aww," I said. "That's so nice of you to say, Mooch."

"Don't mention it," he said and closed his eyes again.

Five minutes later, Brutus walked in through the pet flap, took one look at Mooch, and demanded, "Why are you in Max's spot?"

"It's all right, Brutus," I said. "Mooch is our honored guest, so he can be in my spot."

"Is that so?" said Brutus, looking much surprised. He frowned at me. "When I'm in your spot, you practically hit me in the snoot. But that's all right. I guess Mooch is your friend, and I'm not." And he stalked off.

"Brutus, you are my friend!" I yelled after him.

"Clearly not!" he yelled back. Then he was gone.

Mooch stared at me. "Are you sure you don't want me to move, Max?"

"Absolutely not. Stay right where you are. I insist."

He shrugged. "If you say so."

For a moment, all was quiet, and then Harriet walked in.

"What's this about Mooch being in Max's spot?" she demanded.

"It's fine," I said. "I've given him permission to be in my spot."

"So he gets permission, and Brutus doesn't? That's not fair, Max!"

"It's all right," said Dooley. "Mooch is our honored guest, so he gets to be in Max's spot. Brutus isn't an honored guest, so he doesn't get that privilege."

Harriet glared at me, then shook her head in disgust and stalked out again.

Mooch sighed. "It could just be me, but I have a feeling you would like me to move, Max."

"I don't," I said emphatically. "In fact, I want you to stay right where you are, Mooch. Don't you move from that spot, you hear? I forbid you."

"But Brutus is upset, and Harriet is upset. I don't want to be that dog, Max."

"You aren't. Brutus and Harriet get upset all the time. It's what they do best. So don't pay any attention to them and just stay where you are."

"It's true," Dooley confirmed. "They do like to get upset about all kinds of stuff. And if there's nothing to get upset about, they'll simply invent something."

"What a crazy way to live," said Mooch as he settled down again and closed his eyes. A moment later, we were all relaxing in our designated spots, and peace had finally descended upon the home. Which is the moment Odelia chose to deposit herself in her own designated spot and announce, "We're going on a stakeout, Max. And you and Dooley are coming."

"A stakeout?" asked Dooley. "Ooh, how exciting!"

"Can I come, too!" asked Mooch.

Once I'd translated the dog's words, Odelia seemed

surprised. "I guess so," she said. "But you have to promise to be quiet. The purpose of a stakeout is to catch the bad guys when they least expect it. So no barking, you hear?"

"I promise!" said Mooch, looking very excited indeed. "Ooh, this is just wonderful! I love a nice stakeout! In fact, I love it!"

I wondered when Mooch would ever have been involved in a stakeout situation but decided not to ask. Simply to see him smiling again and happy was enough to invite him to a dozen stakeouts if they had this effect on him.

As for me, I was probably the least excited of all those present. When it became clear that we would stake out the cul-de-sac that night, hoping the hooligans would return so that we could identify Bill Taylor's killer, I became even less excited. Spending the night in a car in a dark cul-de-sac, hoping a couple of young punks would show up and make trouble, was not my idea of a fun evening!

However, since I couldn't express this opinion, I decided to go along with the plan. Hopefully, luck would be on our side, and the killer would show up. But in my experience, it might take several nights before these kids returned to the cul-de-sac and resumed their old ways.

CHAPTER 15

If a passerby happened to glance into the old red Peugeot parked along the entrance to the cul-de-sac, they would have been surprised to find a woman with long blonde hair, a powerfully built man with shoulder-length brown hair, and no less than five pets in the backseat: four cats and one bulldog. Chase hadn't been overly keen on the idea of bringing along all of his wife's cats plus the dog they had recently taken in, but they couldn't very well leave Harriet and Brutus at home and bring me and Dooley. Conversely, they couldn't do the opposite either. And so it was all or nothing as far as Odelia was concerned, who liked to keep the peace in the home by awarding all of her cats an equal amount of attention.

I have to say I wasn't all that happy with the arrangement either, but then I'm a city kitty, and I was feeling a little cramped there in the backseat squeezed in between Brutus and Mooch. Also, the level of hostility between our guest and Brutus was quite palpable in the confined space of the car, and frankly, I had no idea how to rectify it. I tried to make light of the situation, but Brutus wasn't having it, and so silence reigned as Odelia and Chase intensely looked up and down the street and generally adjusted to their own limited space as well.

Chase had decided not to organize the stakeout in his own squad car, as the hooligans might recognize it as a police vehicle. And so he had picked Marge's old Peugeot instead, knowing it wouldn't stand out, and they wouldn't pay any notice to one more car parked along the street.

We had been sitting there for about half an hour when I suddenly got a cramp in my left paw, and as I tried to get rid of the cramp, I thought I saw someone approach. It looked like a kid on a mountain bike, and as he passed, I saw that he was wearing a hoodie. No orange sneakers, though. Odelia and Chase had noticed the same thing and shared a look of excitement. A good start to the evening, they seemed to think.

"What's with all the wriggling?" asked Brutus.

"I've got a cramp in my left paw," I told him.

"You have to bite down on it," Mooch advised. "Or stick a pin in it."

"Do you want me to dig my claw into your paw, Max?" asked Brutus sweetly. "That might do the trick."

"No, I do not want you to dig your claw into my paw, Brutus," I said. "Thank you very much."

"Just trying to help," said Brutus. "Though maybe you want to ask your new best friend Mooch, since apparently he's more important to you than we are."

"Oh, not again with that!" I said. "Mooch is a friend, just like you are my friend. And I like you both equally."

"Even though we've been friends for years, and Mooch just showed up this morning?"

"Yes," I said. "You can't put a quantifier on friendship," I explained.

"And I think you can," said Harriet. "Take me and Mooch,

for instance. We're also friends, but even though I like Mooch, I'm never going to be as close to him as I am to Brutus, who's my very best friend."

"I would like to hope that we're a little bit more than just friends," Brutus grumbled.

"Of course we are more than just friends, sugar britches. I'm just trying to make a point."

"Look, if y'all don't want me here, just say the word and I'm gone," said Mooch, who was starting to get a little annoyed by all these insinuations flying around.

"It's not that we don't want you here, Mooch," said Brutus, who must have remembered that his human obviously was very fond of Mooch and had personally invited him into our home. "It's just that Max seems to have singled you out for preferential treatment, way more than he ever did for me, even though we have known each other for years."

"Come as a guest, stay as a friend, and leave as family," said Dooley. "Mooch may have arrived as a guest, but now he's our friend, and soon he will be family. Isn't that how the saying goes?"

Brutus didn't seem to agree, but I most certainly did. In the short amount of time we had known the bulldog, he had grown on me. Although the couch incident still rankled. But then I guess that's me and the sort of mental rigidity I tend to suffer from.

"Okay, fine," said Brutus finally. "I guess I have been a little harsh on you, Mooch. And for that, I apologize. But you have to understand that I'm not used to entertaining guests, and so I probably overreacted."

"Apology accepted," said Mooch. "And if you look out now, you might see an interesting sight."

We did look outside as he had told us, and we weren't disappointed. From behind us, a group of kids on bicycles and motorcycles had approached and moved past us in the direction of the cul-de-sac. Clearly, the gang was back. At first, they sort of moved back and forth, checking out their old stomping grounds, but when they finally were satisfied that the police presence had gone, they returned and gathered by a bench that had been placed near a green enclave. I couldn't imagine the town council had placed it there for the benefit of these kids, but they evidently thought otherwise, and now squatted on top of the bench, their feet on the seat, and took out cans of beer and started smoking cigarettes that didn't exactly look like cigarettes at all. When a car passed, they threw a can of beer at the car, which bounced off the hood and sprayed the windshield with the fizzy beverage, causing the driver to speed up so they could get away from the young punks. They laughed and high-fived, clearly happy with this new game they'd invented.

"We should arrest them now," Chase said through gritted teeth. "Disturbing the peace, substance abuse, harassment. I could name a few more things."

"First, let's find out if anyone of them is wearing orange sneakers," Odelia suggested.

And so we all craned our necks to determine if one of the kids was the orange-sneakered killer who had murdered Bill Taylor. But much to our disappointment, none of the kids had decided to adopt this powerful fashion statement.

"No such luck," said Odelia finally.

"Maybe he'll show up," said Chase.

"Let's hope so."

And so we settled in for the duration and watched as the kids threw more beer cans at passing cars, tried to wrench a piece of wood from the bench, got into a fist fight, and rolled around the street kicking each other and generally making an absolute nuisance of themselves.

"Now I understand why the people who live here don't

like these kids very much," said Dooley. "They are very annoying, aren't they, Max?"

"I'd say so," I agreed. Though annoying wasn't the word I would have used.

We'd been there for about an hour, but of the orange-sneakered one, there was no trace. At long last, a police car arrived, and Odelia looked up. "Did you send a message to headquarters?"

"Nope," said Chase. "One of the residents must have called it in."

"This should be interesting," said Brutus, craning his neck to take everything in.

The police car now approached the small crew of kids, and one of the officers rolled down his window to address them. But instead of racing away on their bikes, as we had expected, they walked up to the car, and moments later, we saw how an exchange took place between the officers inside the car and the kids. A clear plastic bag containing what looked like little white pills passed from the kids to the officers, and a small wad of cash went the other direction.

"Well, I'll be damned," said Chase, who immediately snapped a couple of shots of the events as they took place right under our noses.

"Do you know these officers?" asked Odelia.

He nodded. "I do, yeah. And if I tell your uncle about this, there will be hell to pay."

The police car drove on, turned at the end of the cul-de-sac, then passed down the street and soon was gone.

"Aren't the police supposed to do something about these kids?" asked Dooley.

"They are, but apparently they're in bed with them," I said.

Dooley laughed. "But Max. They're in a car! How can they be in bed?"

"It's just an expression, Dooley," I said. "It means they're working together."

"Corrupt cops," Brutus grunted. "There's nothing I hate more than corrupt cops."

It had come as something of a shock to see these cops and these kids work together so well. It certainly seemed to give Chase food for thought. And as he called his boss to give him the bad news, it was clear that Uncle Alec wasn't pleased either. And since apparently the killer was a no-show, Chase finally decided that enough was enough and called in the cavalry. In a mere five minutes, several police vehicles arrived and blocked the street. The kids, unable to escape, went in the opposite direction and raced straight at the houses at the end, then navigated the pathways and small strips of lawn separating the houses and were soon gone.

The cops got out of their cars and chased after them, and so did Odelia and Chase. The only ones who stayed put were the five of us, and since we felt a little silly staying on the sidelines like this, we decided to join the fray and soon were in hot pursuit of the hoodlums who had been terrorizing the neighborhood for the past couple of months. Mooch, especially, seemed to be in his element as he charged forward like a jousting knight of old. I could hardly keep up. Then again, I'm built for comfort, not speed. But since cats can really move when they need to, and those kids had to scale a fence and were forced to leave their bikes behind, we soon were hot on their trail.

I wasn't sure what the agreed upon procedure was when we finally did catch up with them, as we hadn't discussed this part of the plan, so I felt forced to improvise. To my left, I saw that Mooch had managed to dig his teeth into the tush of the nearest punk, and so I decided it was a fine example to follow and did the same with my quarry. And so it was that when the officers finally managed to corner those kids, five of them had punctured buttocks, courtesy of the five of us doing the honors. Mooch, to his credit, hung on the longest, and it took some persuading for him to let go. Apart from a predilection for bones, he seemed to have developed a new skill as a police dog.

We were near the community gardens at that point, and as the arrests were made, I marveled once again about the short distance between the cul-de-sac and these gardens. Which made it all the more plausible that one of these kids was responsible for Bill Taylor's murder. And having done my bit in the furtherance of law and order, I returned happy in the knowledge of a job well done.

The taste of sweaty young butt in my mouth was something I had to accept as a small price to pay for doing what was right.

CHAPTER 16

The Hampton Cove PD had a nice haul that night. A dozen so-called hooligans had been arrested for disturbing the peace and other major or minor infractions, two police officers had been suspended pending an investigation into corruption and criminal possession of a controlled substance, and four cats and a dog had their first taste of teenagers and didn't want more. The only regretful aspect of the evening was that the killer of Bill Taylor was most probably not among those arrests. Though Chase, who had read Norman Vincent Peale's book about the power of positive thinking, still held high hopes that he could get one of the dozen arrestees accountable for that particular crime also.

We had left home feeling a little dispirited and also in a sort of fractious mood but returned glorious and thoroughly happy with ourselves and our achievements. And since apparently digging one's teeth into the backsides of a group of good-for-nothing kids creates a bond, on the way back home Brutus and Mooch actually shared a pleasant conversation about the ins and outs of how to conduct a successful stakeout. If they kept this up, they could record a how-to video for YouTube and become famous.

But frankly speaking, I was too exhausted to listen to what they were saying, and as soon as I put my paws on the backseat of Marge's tiny Peugeot, I'm ashamed to admit that I promptly fell asleep. I think I may have dreamed of hoodlums jumping over fences, not unlike counting sheep, but I'm not sure. Oddly enough, by the time I woke up, I wasn't in the car anymore but lying in my favorite spot on the couch. Odelia must have carried me over, I thought, and when I opened my eyes, I saw that Mooch was lying on the other side of the couch, and in between us lay Dooley, Harriet, and Brutus, all snoring away to their heart's content.

Maybe instead of family therapy, therapists across the globe should try sending their warring couples on stakeouts and have them chase suspects. It might fix their broken marriages.

But then I fell asleep once again and didn't wake up until the next morning. We even skipped cat choir that night, which was understandable since we'd had quite the eventful night. At the breakfast table, Chase was full of beans and talking about the night he spent interviewing those kids. He'd taken a break after a while, seeing as they wouldn't budge on the topic of that murder. Oddly enough they also denied ever having destroyed any of the cul-de-sac residents' flower beds. Not that it mattered, as he figured they were all lying through their teeth. And so after he'd returned home to catch a few winks he'd ventured out again to try to get more information out of them. As it was, he certainly had enough on those neighborhood menaces to put them in front of a judge, but that wasn't enough for the detective, who desperately wanted to solve that murder.

Odelia decided to go into the office that day since she was behind on some of her deadlines for the articles she needed to write, and she asked if we wanted to tag along or if we had other plans. I told her maybe we'd stay home and rest and recuperate from all of last night's excitement. And also, I felt I needed to think and try to puzzle together some of the events as they'd occurred, and to do that, I needed some peace and quiet. And even though Odelia's office is fairly quiet, she does get a lot of phone calls and also people laying claim to her attention and her time, so home was probably the best option for us. Besides, I had a feeling Mooch wouldn't appreciate being left alone in a house he barely knew, so it might be best if we stuck around and kept him company.

He may have had a fun time chasing crooks last night, but that didn't mean he was over his human murdering his other humans. Maybe he would never fully recover from such a tragic event.

Brutus and Harriet had left early to head into town, so it was just me, Dooley, and Mooch who stayed behind after Chase and Odelia had left for work. Grace was at daycare, Marge was at the library, Gran and Tex were at the doctor's office, and as soon as the typical business of the start of the day had passed, the house gradually turned nice and quiet, and I gave myself up to thought.

Though it didn't take long for the mailbox to rattle when the postwoman pushed a few letters through the slot, then for the phone to ring, and for the pet flap to flap when Harriet and Brutus walked in again, then out again. All in all, a typical morning at Casa Odelia.

"Okay, so tell me what you're thinking, Max," said Dooley after he had been studying me for a while. "You know you always think better when you have a sparring partner."

It was true. Sometimes these ideas only ripen when you can discuss them with a trusted friend. And since Mooch was

PURRFECT IMPASSE

also lending me a listening ear, I decided to take Dooley up on his offer.

"So we are dealing with three separate cases, correct?"

"Correct," said Mooch, sitting up a little straighter. He didn't know this game, but he seemed to be willing to give it a chance.

"The first one is Paul Römer who first held up a dozen convenience stores and gas stations and then returned home to murder his entire family. Oddly enough, we haven't been able to find the money he stole, so where did that go?" I held up my paws. "We don't know."

"No, we don't," said Mooch happily. His tongue was wagging, a sign he liked this game more and more.

"What we do know is that not all was well in the Römer household. They urgently needed money to pay for Hector's treatment, and they needed a lot of it. Rumor has it the treatment was going to cost hundreds of thousands of dollars, money they simply didn't have. A fundraiser had been set up but was sabotaged by a person or persons unknown, causing their hope of a positive outcome to dwindle. Selling the house wasn't the solution as they already had two mortgages attached to the property and basically they were at the end of their rope. Maria had told her friend Dolores they had a solution, which may have been that string of robberies Paul engaged in. Though according to the information we got from the convenience stores and gas stations he held up, he netted no more than twenty thousand. In other words, not enough to pay for the treatment."

"And so he shot his wife and son and himself," said Mooch.

"Possibly," I allowed. "There are other aspects that we have to consider. One is that male voice Rita the turtle overheard saying 'Please don't leave me,' and also the scream she heard. This was at seven-thirty."

"But what's the connection?" asked Dooley.

"We don't know if there is one," I conceded. "There is also the fact that the house of the Campbells was broken into and that the door Mikaela had closed was open. However, nothing was stolen as far as she could tell."

"Very mysterious," Mooch agreed. "Go on, please, Max."

"Furthermore, we also know there existed several feuds. One was between Raquel Williams and the Römers, having to do with the chocolate chip cookie recipe that Jim Ward stole from Maria and gave to Raquel, who proceeded to offer cookies baked according to her own family recipe to Maria, who wasn't happy about that. Raquel also stole Maria's cookies at the summer picnic and sold them at a bake sale. Maria found out about that and told Dolores that she was horrified when she found out but didn't want to make a fuss. And there's also the fundraiser set up by Alice Morgan, which subsequently was successfully sabotaged through a social media campaign claiming that Hector Römer wasn't sick, had never been sick, and that the Römers intended to use the money to take a vacation in Europe. Maria told Dolores that she suspected that Raquel was behind the gossip campaign. But when questioned by Chase, Raquel protested her innocence."

"I believed her," said Dooley. "But if she didn't sabotage the fundraiser, who did?"

"No idea," I admitted. "Next is Jim Ward, who also had a feud going on with the Römers, only in his case it was with Paul, not Maria. The business with the tree and the flowers. We don't need to go into all of that again, but suffice it to say that there was a lot of bad blood between some of these neighbors, which may have contributed to the tragedy that occurred two nights ago."

"So what about the death of my humans?" asked Mooch. "Is that connected to the Römer case or not?"

"I'm not sure," I confessed. "But let's look at the facts. Mark Turner confessed to murdering his parents, even though you claim that he couldn't have done it because he's not a murderer."

"He isn't," Mooch confirmed. "That boy doesn't have a bad bone in his body, and trust me, I know all about bones, Max. I'm probably a bone specialist."

"I know you are, Mooch," I said warmly. "And I'll take it into consideration. What we also know is that on the morning that the Turners were murdered, Jim Ward saw a hooded figure walk across the community gardens. It was raining hard, so he couldn't get a good look, but he thought it was probably a man."

"Was he wearing orange sneakers?" asked Dooley suddenly.

"I'm afraid Jim didn't say, but it is possible that he was. In which case, Jim may have seen his friend Bill Taylor's killer."

"It must be those young punks again," said Dooley with a shake of the head. "They do keep causing trouble."

"Murdering a person probably qualifies as more than causing trouble," I said. "Though it's true that they're still the main suspects for Mr. Taylor's murder."

"So do you think all three of these cases are connected somehow?" asked Mooch.

"I do, yes," I said, surprising myself, for I hadn't really made the connections yet. But a hunch told me that they were definitely there, hidden in the evidence that we had gathered so far.

Suddenly, Dooley had an idea. "The gun that killed Paul Römer and his wife and son, was it his?"

"It was," I confirmed. "He was the license holder."

"And his fingerprints were on the gun?"

"They were."

"Oh," said my friend. "Too bad."

I smiled. "Yeah, too bad."

"Why? What were you thinking, Dooley?" asked Mooch.

"Oh, I suddenly wondered if maybe someone else had killed the Römers and then tried to make it look like a murder-suicide. But if it was his gun, and his prints on the gun..."

"And also the gunpowder residue that was on his hand points to him firing the gun," I added for good measure.

Dooley threw up his paws. "Okay, then I don't see how this case could possibly be connected to the other two cases, Max. Unless somehow Paul Römer murdered Bill Taylor?"

"He didn't, since Mr. Taylor died early the next morning, probably around the same time the Turners were killed."

"I guess dead men can't kill people," Dooley said sadly. He stared at me. "I really don't see it, Max. I don't."

"To be honest, I don't either, Dooley. At least not yet."

"You'll get there," Mooch assured me. "You may have a hunch about these three cases being connected, and I have a hunch that your hunch is correct and that you'll figure it out."

"Thanks for the vote of confidence, Mooch," I said, though he was definitely more convinced of my eventual success than I was.

The door opened and Odelia walked in. "We're going to interview Bill Taylor's sister," she announced. "Wanna come?"

CHAPTER 17

Caroline Parker was probably the same age as her brother. Her gray hair was tucked away in a bun, and she was dressed in a tasteful style. We met at a café in town since she didn't live in Hampton Cove but in Boston and had come down to make the funeral arrangements and to clean out her brother's apartment. She seemed sad but not overwhelmingly so, and I had the impression that she and her brother hadn't seen a lot of each other these past couple of years.

"Bill used to live in Boston, where our family is from," she explained as she took a sip from her mint tea. "Like all of his siblings he worked for the family company—we're in the denim industry, one of the major players—as CFO. But about ten years ago, we had to let him go after it transpired that he'd been embezzling money from the company and transferring it to his personal account. My uncle who's the CEO had no choice but to let Bill go, but we did manage to keep it out of the papers. Bill moved away to Hampton Cove and lived a quiet life, not drawing too much attention to himself. I think he was mostly ashamed about what he'd done."

"But why did he steal from his own family?" asked Odelia.

Caroline considered the question. "What I tell you has to stay between us," she insisted.

"This is a murder investigation, Mrs. Parker," Chase pointed out, "so we can't possibly make that promise."

"Mh," said the woman and stalled for time by taking another sip from her tea. Finally, she nodded. "I'll tell you what happened. Bill is gone now, so I don't see the point of keeping it a secret. He got involved with a woman who turned out to be a prostitute and proceeded to blackmail him. She had filmed the two of them together, and since Bill was married at the time, and also a member of a prominent family, the scandal would have been too much for him. So he paid her off, just as she demanded. Only she kept coming back for more, and to make sure his wife didn't find out, he couldn't take the money from their joint account, so he decided to steal from the company instead. When an internal audit revealed the theft, he came clean. It ended his marriage, and also his career, but at least he was finally free from this demonic woman. As it later transpired, she had been working for a local mobster, and when she failed to deliver, he cut her from his payroll. Literally. Her body was found floating in the Mystic River. She'd been stabbed to death."

Odelia and Chase shared a look. "Stabbed?" asked Chase.

"Yeah, just like Bill." She raised a meaningful eyebrow.

"Is it possible—"

"That this same mobster found out about Bill's whereabouts and came after him?" She shrugged. "It's possible, of course, but unlikely. Rumor had it that this woman my brother was involved with had decided to work her own scam and had skimmed some money off the top when her clients paid her. Yeah, Bill wasn't the only one who'd fallen under her spell. She was working several targets at the same time. According to the police, it wasn't losing Bill that sealed her fate but the fact that she had been double-crossing her employer."

"So unlikely they would come after Bill after all these years," said Odelia.

"That's just my opinion," said the woman. "You're the police, so you'll have to find out what happened. All I can say is that my brother was happy here. He'd lived a high-profile life in Boston, working a demanding job, and locked in a loveless marriage. Somehow by losing all of that he found himself, and the last time we spoke he said he was very happy pottering about his garden and living an anonymous life."

"He didn't have kids?"

"No kids. He was too busy for that." She smiled a wry smile. "I think he would have made a great dad, not when he was still Boston Bill, but definitely as Hampton Cove Bill. But of course, he was probably too old to start a family, and also, he didn't seem interested in that part of his life."

"So can you think of anyone else who might have held a grudge against your brother?" asked Odelia. "Or someone he got into a fight with?"

Caroline shook her head. "Like I said, he was happy here, and if he did get into a conflict with anyone, he didn't tell me about it. But I didn't get that impression. He kept a low profile and lived a low-key life, and that's exactly how he liked it."

Chase and Odelia sat back, and Chase said that they had arrested several young suspects last night who had been terrorizing a neighborhood, and that he had a strong suspicion that one of them had killed Bill, possibly in a case of mistaken identity. He also told Caroline that they were conducting house searches for all the suspects and hoped to turn up something to connect them to the murder, preferably the shoes that the killer had been wearing and that a witness had seen.

They said their goodbyes, and Caroline expressed a fervent wish that her brother's killer would be brought to justice. "He was basically a good man," she said. "He made one big mistake by falling for the wrong woman, but somehow he managed to turn his life around and lead a happy life in the aftermath. He didn't deserve to die like this, not after all he'd been through, and considering how happy he was living here in Hampton Cove, which he said was possibly the loveliest town in the country, with the kindest, friendliest people he had ever met."

"We'll catch the person that did this," Chase promised.

"Please keep me informed," she said as she pressed his hand warmly. "And now if you'll please excuse me, I have a funeral to arrange."

We watched her leave, her head ramrod straight, and carrying herself with dignity and poise, in spite of the great loss that had afflicted her.

"Oh, in other news," said Chase, as he took a seat again with Odelia, "we heard back from Facebook."

"Oh? So who set up that hateful campaign?"

"You'll never guess. The Römers themselves!"

"What! But that's impossible."

"An IP address never lies, babe. The router those vile messages originated from has been identified as belonging to the Römers. So turns out they were orchestrating the campaign to sabotage their own fundraiser themselves."

"That doesn't make any sense," said Odelia. "No sense at all."

"I know it doesn't. But that's what the evidence bears out, so looks like Raquel Williams is in the clear, just like she told us. She didn't do it."

They both got up from their respective chairs, Odelia to return to the office, and Chase to the station. As far as Dooley and myself and Mooch were concerned, we decided to go for a little walk. Clearly, this information had shocked my friends, and also my humans, and a nice brisk walk would hopefully give us the oxygen to make our little gray cells make sense of what we'd just heard. Adding to our little pile of evidence, now we also knew that Bill Taylor had been the victim of a scam set up by the Boston Mob and had escaped to Hampton Cove to get away from his past. And we also knew that the Römers themselves had sabotaged their chance to enter their son into their expensive Swiss clinic. Or as Dooley explained it: "What a mess, Max!"

CHAPTER 18

Dooley, Mooch, and I soon found ourselves drifting into Kingman's ken. Kingman is our large feline friend who lives above the General Store. As is his habit, he was seated in front of his human's store in the center of Main Street and looking out across the world, studying the passersby, and chatting with any cat who walked by. Kingman is more or less Hampton Cove's unofficial feline mayor and pretty much knows everything and everyone there is to know in our small town. When we arrived, he wasn't alone but chatting with Harriet and Brutus, who had also decided to go for a little stroll. When they saw us arrive, a smile slid up their faces.

"Hey, Mooch," said Brutus, clearly having come to terms with the arrival in our midst of a canine of the bulldog persuasion.

"Hey, Brutus, Harriet," said Mooch, then eyed Kingman a little uncertainly.

"I'm Kingman," said the large cat, introducing himself with customary amiability. "And you must be Mooch. I've heard so much about you that I feel like I've known you forever, buddy."

Mooch smiled. "And I've heard a lot about you, Kingman."

In other words, the meeting was entirely cordial. No cats were chased into trees by recalcitrant dogs, and generally a good time was had by all. We even shot the breeze for almost twenty minutes before I remembered the problems we were faced with. And so I put it to the others in no uncertain terms.

"We're still no closer to solving the murder of Bill Taylor, you guys. Those kids that Chase arrested last night don't seem to have had anything to do with the murder. Or at least they're not admitting to it. And also, we just discovered that the Römers sabotaged their own fundraiser, destroying their only realistic chance to cure their boy and save his life."

This had my friends stumped, just as it had us stumped. Now who in their right mind would set up a fundraiser and then expertly throw a monkey wrench in the works? That didn't make any sense at all and had me baffled to a great degree.

"I think I might know the answer," said Dooley. "They probably felt guilty about accepting all of that money. Some people are like that, you know. They're nervous about accepting a gift from other people. Remember when Marge got that nice necklace for her birthday? She even said it out loud: you shouldn't have done it, Tex. So she wanted it, but she didn't want it. And I even thought that Tex was going to take it back to the store, but of course he didn't."

"That's not the same thing, Dooley," said Harriet. "People love to receive gifts, but it's just a formula they use to show their appreciation. Like when Brutus gives me a gift, I could say the same thing: 'Oh, you shouldn't have done it, smoochie poo.'" She thought for a moment. "Then again, I would never say that."

"No, you'd probably say: 'Is there more where this came from?'" said Kingman and laughed loudly at his own joke. But Harriet wasn't laughing, so he quickly stifled his laugh in his paw.

"I think I know what might be playing out here," said Brutus. "These Römers were simply fooling everyone. Their kid wasn't sick and had never been sick. They simply created this story about this Swiss clinic to extract as much money from their friends and relatives and work colleagues as they could. But then at some point, they must have started feeling guilty when all of that money was starting to come in, and so they decided to pull the plug. Only they couldn't admit to what they'd done, so to save face, they simply sabotaged their own campaign, causing it to shut down and the money to be returned." He held up his paws. "Everybody happy!"

"Not the Römers, apparently, for Paul Römer decided to go on a robbery spree and then proceeded to kill his entire family," Kingman pointed out. "So there are definitely holes in that story of yours, buddy boy."

"Yeah, I guess there are," said Brutus, rubbing his chin. "Okay, so how about this? Paul Römer was the one behind the scheme to get the money, but his wife was the one with the qualms. So when her husband wasn't looking, she decided to nuke the fundraiser he'd set up. And then since he wouldn't give up on his dream of using his son to get rich quickly, he robbed those stores. Only when he got home he found his wife extremely upset about what he'd done, so they had this major blowout, which ended with him shooting his wife, then himself."

"What about his son?" I asked. "What father would shoot his own son?"

But Brutus had his answer ready. "Collateral damage," he said simply. "He wanted to shoot his wife, but not being an expert shot, he killed his kid instead, then decided to finish the job by killing his wife and turning the gun on himself. There is your answer, Max. Now run to Odelia and give her the solution, cause I can see you're eager to."

But I shook my head. "I'm sorry, but I don't buy it, Brutus. I mean, I just don't see it, you know. From all accounts, the Römers were a devoted and loving couple. I don't see a fight that ends with the entire family lying dead."

"It happens. People snap and do crazy stuff. Why, only last week Shanille went totally berserk when I couldn't hit the right note right off the bat. She even called me a few choice names that I chose not to respond to. But it was totally uncalled for and I could have unloaded on her. But fortunately for her, I'm a gentlecat and I'm always in complete control of my emotions."

We all grinned at him. "Yeah, right," said Kingman, wording our collective sentiment best.

"No, but it's true! I'm like a ninja that way. You can tell me anything to my face and I simply will not respond. Here, try it. Call me an opprobrious name."

He was addressing me for some reason, and I shook my head. "Let's not."

"No, but please do. I want you to see how impervious I am to verbal abuse. Your slings and arrows can't affect me."

"Okay, if you really insist," I said reluctantly. "Brutus, you're ugly."

He winced a little but otherwise didn't respond.

"Hey, I like this game," said Kingman. He turned to our friend. "Brutus, you're so ugly my eyes hurt every time I look at you."

I could see he was having trouble, for his face was working, and his breathing turned a little erratic. But still, he didn't explode.

"Brutus, you're so ugly you make onions cry!" said Mooch, deciding to join the fun.

"You're so ugly Farmer Giles uses you as a scarecrow," said Dooley with a grin.

"You're so ugly when you look in a mirror it cracks," said Harriet.

"You're so ugly," said Kingman, "you don't need a mask for Halloween."

"You're so ugly—"

Suddenly a sort of loud roar seemed to rise up somewhere in our vicinity. It sounded like the roar of a monster of the deep, and we all searched around for the source of the sound before realizing it was actually Brutus who was screaming so loud that even Wilbur Vickery walked out of his store to see what was going on.

"I hate you guys!" Brutus bellowed, shaking his fists in fury. "I hate all of you!"

So much for his extreme powers of self-control.

"Brutus, stud muffin, I thought you said you were a ninja!" said Harriet, surprised by this outburst.

Suddenly he burst into tears and placed his head on his true love's shoulder. "Am I really so ugly?" he wailed. "Tell me it isn't true-ue-ue-ueee!"

"It isn't true," said Harriet, patting him on the back. "We were just kidding!"

"It's a kids' game," I pointed out. "Kids love these 'you're so ugly' jokes so we decided we would try it on you, to test your amazing ninja powers of self-control."

"I failed, didn't I?" he sniffled. "I don't have any ninja powers!" Then he suddenly turned on me. "Which just goes to show, Max, that anyone can crack! Even me—the strongest cat on the block! And if I can crack under a couple of 'you're so ugly' jokes, I'm pretty sure Paul Römer could also crack, and he did!"

It was certainly a compelling argument, and I had no recourse. Of course, Paul Römer could have cracked, and obviously he did, but there were still some elements about the whole affair that didn't sit well with me. But since Brutus was in quite a state, we all rallied round and consoled him to the best of our abilities. Even Mooch chipped in and gave him pats on the back. Brutus may be the strongest cat on the block, but his ego is as delicate as anyone's.

"The same thing happened last week," Kingman said once Brutus was more or less himself again. "This customer came into the store and started complaining about the price of the tomatoes. Said he'd never seen tomatoes as ugly as the ones Wilbur was selling and asking such outrageous prices. So this whole fight erupted over these tomatoes, which ended with Wilbur throwing a tomato at the guy's head. At which point, the guy picked up a ripe one and threw it at Wilbur's head. I had to duck as suddenly this massive food fight broke out, and when all was said and done the store looked a righteous mess, and so did both Wilbur and the customer!" He shook his head. "And all over the price of tomatoes, if you please. I'm telling you, humans are nuts."

"They are nuts," Mooch agreed. "They'll kill each other over a trifle. Like with my humans. Some bad person must have been upset over some ill-perceived slight and decided to get even."

We all looked at the bulldog with compassion, for it was pretty obvious that no 'bad person' had killed his humans over an ill-perceived slight. Mark had. But then, as the conversation turned to other topics, suddenly I found myself reflecting on Kingman's words, and for the first time since this string of terrible events had started, I thought I saw a light at the end of the tunnel. And the worst part was that it had all stared me right in the face from the very beginning! Gah. What a fool I'd been. I could have solved these murders in a heartbeat if only I'd been smart enough to listen.

Then again, since there were still a few loose ends to tie

up, I decided that there was no time like the present and whispered to my friend Dooley that if he had a moment to spare and could drag himself away from the no doubt fascinating conversation about tomatoes and the frailty of the human ego, he could accompany me to Odelia and present her with a compelling case.

Much to my relief, he immediately said yes, and so we said our goodbyes to our friends and went in search of our human. We had work to do, and more importantly: we had a killer to catch. A killer who had killed six people and no doubt would kill again if necessary!

CHAPTER 19

Mike Campbell couldn't help but feel a touch of concern after what he'd heard from his neighbor. Alice had told him in confidence that the police were close to a breakthrough in the murder case that had rocked their small community. The man found murdered in his own garden shed was revealed as a member of a very prominent Boston family who had vowed to leave no stone unturned to identify their relative's killer and bring him to justice. And here he had thought all along that the man was nothing but a lowly bum, a seedy local pensioner who enjoyed nothing more than to potter around his little garden and watch his tomatoes grow. Turned out the guy was a millionaire many times over!

Just shows you how wrong you can be about people. What was even more disturbing was that the murder had been witnessed. The police weren't revealing who the witness was, no doubt in an effort to protect their safety. The only good thing was that the witness hadn't actually made a positive identification of the killer. But even so, when faced with the person, it might jar their memory, and they might point the finger at the hapless murderer they had seen that morning.

Mike could just imagine how the police had this witness safely locked away somewhere in a safe house, making sure Bill Taylor's killer couldn't come anywhere near them. And to top off the list of bad news, Alice had also revealed that the police had tracked down another witness who had identified the shoes the killer had been wearing! A pair of bright orange sneakers, she had said, then had darted a curious look at him, making the hairs at the back of his neck stand up. "Don't you own a pair of bright orange sneakers, Mike?"

He had laughed what he had hoped was a careless laugh and said, "Oh, I threw those away ages ago. They were totally worn out. Got them in a sale, you know. Terrible quality."

She had given him a strange look, and somehow he had known that she knew. How she knew he did not know, but it was obvious that she did. So he had quickly returned home, dug out those treacherous sneakers from the back of his shoe cabinet, shoved them into a plastic bag, and had opened the back door, preparatory to going for a run through the field that lay behind the house so he could safely discard the shoes. But just as he was about to set off, suddenly a man appeared, as if spirited out of thin air. It was that beefy cop, the one built like a bodybuilder. He eyed him intently.

"Going somewhere, Mike?" asked the cop.

He gave the man a pleasant smile. "I was just going for a run, detective."

"I don't think so," said the cop.

For a moment, he thought about rushing the man and digging his head into his stomach, but then another person showed up. Odelia Kingsley, that annoying busybody of a reporter. And as he backtracked in the direction of the house, he almost bumped into yet another cop, this one dressed in the official Hampton Cove PD uniform. And as he glanced around, he saw that he was surrounded by the law. They were everywhere! And as he glanced down, he saw that those horrible cats were also there. That fat orange one and the small gray one. They were looking as intently at him as the cops were. Oh, curse those stupid cats and their stupid ways! For a moment, he considered trying to break through the line of cops, like a Running Back in a football game, but then a familiar voice sounded behind him. It was Mikaela, and she didn't sound pleased.

"Is it true, Mike? Did you kill that poor bum in his garden house?"

"Don't believe a word they tell you, Mikaela," he warned his wife of twenty-five years. "I didn't do it!"

"Oh, Mike," she said brokenly. "Why? Why did you do it?"

He glanced behind her and saw that even their two turtles were watching closely, as if anticipating his every move.

"Yeah, why did you do it, Mike?" asked the cop.

"I did not, all right?" he said. "I had nothing to do with the whole sordid business. Probably some other bum killed him over a bottle of wine. You know what these winos are like. Animals, each and every one of them." He'd broken out in a cold sweat as he grasped that bag with the shoes tightly.

"What have you got in that bag, Mike?" asked Mrs. Kingsley.

"Nothing," he said. "Just some old junk."

"Hand it over," said the cop, and there was steel in his voice.

So he handed it over. The cop looked in the bag, saw the shoes, and whistled through his teeth. "Nice pair of sneakers. Very bright and very orange." He handed the bag to a member of his team, who proceeded to take out what Mike knew was an evidence bag, sealed it, and left the scene, presumably to hand the bag over to a forensic specialist, just like you saw on those cop shows on television. Apparently these days they could prove anything just by looking at a speck of dust under a microscope. And since he hadn't exactly been extra careful when he got rid of that old geezer, they'd probably find lots and lots of evidence.

"It... it was self-defense," he said finally, trying a different tack. "He attacked me, that old wino! I had no choice." He glanced at his wife. "Honey, you have to believe me. I was just going about my business, and suddenly this old guy attacked me! If I hadn't done what I did, he would have killed me for sure!"

"And what about the Römers, Mike?" said Detective Kingsley. "Did they also attack you? Or the Turners?"

God, so they knew about that, did they? Which is when he finally broke down and said curtly, "I'm not saying another word until I speak to my lawyer."

Behind him, his wife burst into tears, his turtles shook their tiny wrinkled heads in dismay, and those infuriating cats simply sat there and stared.

CHAPTER 20

"Okay, so I don't understand anything," Harriet confessed. "Why did this guy murder all of his neighbors, Max?"

"Yeah, and how did you figure it out?" Brutus added.

We were all seated on the porch swing in Marge and Tex's backyard, with the family enjoying a nice barbecue while their feline counterparts huddled on the swing, eager to partake in the feast. Tex was busy whipping up precious morsels of meat on the grill, and generally the mood was festive and happy. The topic of conversation, as was to be expected, was the shock revelation that Mike Campbell had murdered no less than six people in the space of one night and one day. And he probably would have gotten away with it if not for his peculiar choice of footwear and the incriminating testimony of his neighbor Jim Ward, who had seen the murderer pass through the community gardens on the day the Turners and Bill Taylor had been killed.

"I think his main motivation was greed," I told my captive audience, which consisted of Dooley, Harriet, Brutus, and also Mooch. Even though Mooch had been reunited with his human Mark Turner, he had decided to stick around for the barbecue, and also my modest little exposé about the events that had shocked quite a few people in our otherwise pleasant little town. "The most important aspect of this case was the fact that the Campbells, after many years of playing the same numbers in the lottery, had finally seen their patience be rewarded. They had won one million dollars, a fantastic sum for a couple who had always been forced to live more frugally than most. They may have lived in a nice house in a nice cul-de-sac, but were not as prosperous as their neighbors. You might even say that they were living above their means to some extent. Mike worked as an accountant, and his wife Mikaela as a cleaning lady. Through a lucky coincidence, they had been able to buy that house, at a price much lower than the market demanded, and had been nervous about revealing their true financial situation to their neighbors ever since. So when they won that lottery, they couldn't believe their luck, and frankly, Mike probably went a little crazy contemplating what they could do with all of that money. After all those years of scrimping and saving, their ship had finally come in, and he was determined to make the most of it."

"He should have given some of it to the Römers," said Dooley. "They could have used that money to save their son."

"That's exactly what Paul Römer thought," I agreed. "But initially the Römers didn't know about their neighbors' lucky lottery win since Mike and Mikaela had vowed to keep it a secret from everybody, lest they ask them to share. Especially the Römers, with their sick son. So that night, when Paul returned from his robbery spree to hide the loot in the community gardens, in one of the empty garden houses, picture his surprise when he saw a light burning in one of the other garden houses and peeking in through the window saw his neighbor. Mike was busy preparing the next phase of a campaign that would see him and Mikaela move up in the world.

"Paul was very much surprised to see Mike Campbell busy with some kind of science experiment. Or at least that's what it looked like to the innocent observer. So he knocked on the door, causing Mike to jump out of his skin, and asked him what he was doing. Mike gave him some innocuous explanation, which is when Paul saw that same lottery ticket, enhanced and framed against the wall of Mike's shed. It was such bad luck, and Mike must have kicked himself for this indulgence, for immediately the conversation turned acrimonious. Paul asked him why he had kept his lottery win a secret and immediately begged him to lend him the money he needed for Hector's treatment. And when Mike didn't respond the way he'd hoped, he got really upset."

"He was desperate," Harriet said, nodding.

"He'd gone on this robbery spree, which hadn't netted him what he'd hoped, and now saw that lottery money as his last hope. So he was determined to do whatever it took to get his hands on that money. Which is why he took out the gun he'd taken along with him for his robberies and told Mike that he was going to sign that money over to him right then and there, or else. Mike, staring into the barrel of that gun, quickly acquiesced, and together they returned to the Römer place, where Maria must have been surprised to see Paul return, not with the loot, but with Mike, held at gunpoint. But just like Paul was determined to get that money off his neighbor, Mike was equally determined to hold on to it. At some point, Paul must have been distracted, and Mike went for the gun. In the struggle, the gun went off and killed Maria. Which is when Mike decided that he was in serious trouble, but instead of backing off, he decided to take things one step further and shot Paul through the temple. That only left Hector, so he put the gun in the dead Paul's hand, pulled the trigger one last time, and left the house after having wiped out all three members of the Römer family, making it look as if Paul had shot his wife and kid and then himself."

"How awful," said Harriet, shaking her head at such heinousness.

"And all because he wanted to hold on to his money," Brutus grunted.

"So what does that have to do with the death of my human?" asked Mooch.

"That's what Mike was doing in that shed," I explained. "With that million dollars in their bank account, the Campbells decided they were moving up in the world by buying the one property they'd had their eye on for a long time. And that property was the old farmhouse that the Turners had fixed up at great expense and was located not all that far from the cul-de-sac where Mike and Mikaela lived. On their daily walks through the countryside, they had passed that house many times and had seen its transformation from an old farmhouse to the gorgeous place that it had become. And they coveted it. Oh, how they wanted it for themselves. Especially Mike. It was his dream home, the one he aspired to possess. He saw the house, the happy couple that lived there, the kid, and he wanted all of that. Only when he knocked on the door with that million dollars in the bank, convinced it would be an easy buy, the Turners turned him down flat. They weren't selling. They had invested not just a small fortune but also their heart and soul and weren't going to part with the house they'd fallen in love with also, and where they were so happy as a family."

"And where I was so very happy," Mooch added sadly.

"And so Mike finally decided that if the Turners weren't willing to sell the house, he was going to take it. And since the only way he could accomplish that was by getting rid of the Turners, that's what he'd do. Which is why he had been carefully planning to murder the couple in cold blood and let Mark take the rap for it. It was the perfect murder, and he had been perfecting his plan in that garden shed of his for several nights in a row, getting the chloroform he needed to knock out Mark, and also the spiked meatball he planned to feed to Mooch to get rid of him."

"Did I eat a spiked meatball?" asked Mooch. "I don't even remember."

"You did," I assured him. "You told us you were asleep when it happened, remember? And Mark told us he woke up next to his parents' bodies, the knife in his hand. That's because you were both drugged. And then when Mark woke up, naturally he thought he had murdered them."

"I didn't," said Mooch. "Didn't I tell you from the start that Mark was innocent? I told you, didn't I? I did!"

"Yeah, you did," said Brutus, patting the bulldog on the back.

"You did good, Mooch," Harriet added. "You're the best friend Mark could have wished for. And if you hadn't been knocked out, Mike wouldn't have stood a chance. Isn't that right, Max?"

"It is," I confirmed. "Which is why it was so vital to Mike's plan to get rid of both Mark and Mooch. Otherwise, he wouldn't have been able to get away with it."

"Only Paul almost ruined things for him by catching him," said Brutus.

"Exactly. And Paul wasn't the only unforeseen circumstance he encountered."

"Bill Taylor?" asked Dooley.

I nodded. "Mike had gone over to the Turner place very early that morning when it was still dark, and after he killed the couple, he hurried back through the fields, hoping not to bump into any witnesses. His plan was to dump his blood-spattered clothes at the shed, then return later to destroy the evidence. This was the reason he'd occupied the garden house, which had been empty for a while, waiting for a new occupant. And also he didn't want his wife to find out, because she wouldn't have approved of his plans. Only when he arrived there after the murder, he suddenly saw a man staring at him in the early morning light. It was Bill Taylor, who loved nothing more than to spend his days in his beloved garden, and who happened to be an early riser."

"So he stabbed him," said Brutus.

"Yeah, he did," I said. "Mike had now killed five people, and he probably figured one more wouldn't matter, as long as he was safe. By this time, it had started to rain, a regular downpour, and as he hurried back to his garden house to get rid of his clothes, he was seen by his neighbor Jim Ward, only this time, he didn't notice that he'd been spotted."

"Or else he would have been forced to kill Jim as well?" said Harriet.

"Yeah, probably," I said.

"So Mr. Ward had a lucky escape," said Brutus.

"But why didn't he get rid of those orange sneakers?" asked Dooley.

"Because he didn't know he'd been seen, and also..." I smiled. "Those shoes were a gift from his wife, and he couldn't bear to destroy them. He did burn the hoodie he'd been wearing and the pants, but he kept the sneakers. And he probably shouldn't have, for forensic examination has determined they were covered with tiny droplets of blood that have positively been matched to Paul Römer, the Turners and Bill Taylor. Which is why Mike tried to get rid of the shoes when he was caught."

Chase and Odelia had coached Alice to draw Mike out by revealing to him that the police were about to make an arrest, and that they had a witness who had seen the murderer wear exactly this type of sneaker. Which is why he was suddenly in such a hurry to destroy the sneakers, something he must have realized he should have done in the first place but didn't have the heart to."

"So how did you figure it out, Max?" Harriet repeated.

"I had this hunch all along that these three cases were connected somehow," I said. "Though for the life of me, I couldn't see how. It was when Kingman mentioned that this human had this big food fight over the price of tomatoes that it dawned on me that the main motive in all of this just possibly might be money. Which is when I suddenly remembered something I'd discarded: that Mike and Mikaela's turtles had revealed that the couple had won the lottery. But since Fifi assured us that Rita was an incorrigible liar, I believed her and figured this whole story about the big lottery win and subsequent move to Florida was nothing but a figment of Rita's imagination. But it wasn't, even though Mike wasn't planning to move to Florida at all, but closer to home."

"Into the Turner place," said Brutus.

"Into my home!" Mooch said.

"Into your home," I agreed. "And so once I had a possible motive, everything quickly fell into place. The murder of the Römers, the attack on the Turners, and also the murder of Bill Taylor and the sighting of the orange-sneakered man. Now all we had to do was to draw out Mike Campbell, and so we did."

"What a dreadful business," said Harriet, and I think she spoke for all of us when she said it. "Just so they could go and live in their dream home, which happened to be someone else's dream home."

"Maybe if they'd just moved to Florida, like Mikaela wanted," said Brutus, "none of this would have happened."

"Oh, but Mikaela wouldn't have minded to live in the

Turner place," I said. "Only she wasn't prepared to go to these lengths to get there. That was all Mike."

"But why, Max?" asked Mooch. "Why did Mike Campbell turn into a killer?"

"That," I said, "is probably a question best answered by a shrink. But it's entirely possible that after seeing his dreams thwarted over and over again, he figured he deserved to get his due."

"And he was prepared to kill six people to do it," Brutus said.

It wasn't a nice state of affairs, but that's how it happened, and if we hadn't stopped him, who knows how many more people Mike might have killed. Clearly, something had snapped in the man, or else he wouldn't have done what he did. But at least now justice would be done, and a great menace had been removed from society.

Odelia walked over and handed us our little morsels of delicious meats, straight from her dad's grill, and rubbed me on the head. She had already thanked me for my services, and so had Chase. And even though I wasn't proud that it had taken me so long to figure it out, I still felt that I'd done my bit in the furtherance of the truth, which filled me with a certain sense of pride.

And so we all tucked in, and so did our humans, and a good time was had by all. Life may not always be fair, but it was at moments like these that I felt we'd certainly been dealt a more than fair hand. The best humans, the best friends, and plenty of delicious grub. What more can one want?

And so after having eaten our fill, our tummies happy and round, we settled in for a nice nap, which in my personal opinion was long overdue! And thus ended another harrowing adventure, brought to a satisfying conclusion.

. . .

"Max?"

"Yes, Dooley?"

"There's one thing I still don't understand."

"What's that?"

"Well, the scream that Rita heard, and the male voice that said, 'Please don't leave me.' What was that all about?"

"Oh, that," I said. "Well, the scream was Maria, when she discovered that her husband had bought an actual gun and was planning to use it for the robberies he'd been planning. I think it's safe to say she wasn't fully on board with that part of the plan, since she abhorred violence. They had a whispered argument in the backyard, and at some point things got so bad Paul begged her not to leave him, which she must have threatened him with. And as it turned out she was right, because the robberies didn't net Paul as much as he had hoped they would. And if Paul hadn't hidden the money, he wouldn't have stumbled upon Mike, and the Römers would still be alive."

"Hector might not have been alive," Harriet pointed out.

"Oh, that's something else I don't understand," said Dooley.

Resigned now that I would never get my nap, I said, "What?"

"Well, the sabotage of the fundraiser. Why would the Römers do that?"

"They didn't. That was all Alice Morgan's doing. Raquel might have had a beef with Maria, and Jim Ward and Paul Römer were engaged in their feud, but Alice and Raquel were also locked in a feud of their own. As Alice told Odelia, she once caught Raquel pinching Fifi when she thought Alice wasn't looking, and vowed revenge for this display of animal cruelty. And so when Alice saw an opportunity to smear Raquel's name, she took it. So she launched that campaign against the Römers, using Raquel's router. Only she was mistaken, and used the Römers' router instead."

"Aren't these routers protected by a password?" asked Brutus.

"They should be protected with a password, but apparently theirs wasn't. And so Alice, in her attempt to point the finger at Raquel, managed to single-handedly destroy Paul and Maria's fundraiser, which she had set up, by the way. She felt fairly certain that Paul and Maria would involve the police, and the trail would lead to Raquel, causing her so much embarrassment that she would have to move away from the cul-de-sac and they'd finally be rid of the woman. The whole thing would attract a lot of attention and give the fundraiser a much-needed boost that would put it over the top. Or so she thought. But the Römers were so demoralized they simply dropped the whole idea of the fundraiser."

"Probably causing Alice much distress," said Harriet.

"Yeah, she felt terrible about what she did, and actually planned to set up a new campaign, and she probably would have succeeded this time, only fate intervened and it was too late."

"Fate didn't intervene," said Mooch. "Mike Campbell did."

"There's one other thing that's not clear to me, Max," said Dooley.

"Yes, Dooley?" I said, starting to feel a little persecuted.

"The break-in at the Campbells. The door that was locked at night by Mikaela and that was unlocked later on, though nothing was stolen."

"Well, that's easy," said Brutus. "Mike forgot to relock it when he returned home. Right, Max?"

"Wrong," I said. "Mike was nothing if not careful, except about those sneakers. So he did lock the door when he returned after murdering the Römers, and snuck into bed again while his wife was still sound asleep. Or so he thought."

As it turned out, Mikaela also had a bad habit. Not nearly as bad as her husband's habit of murdering people who stood in the way of acquiring his dream home, but definitely annoying. She had gotten into the habit of sleepwalking and wandering all over the house. When the mood struck her, she even ventured outside. Which is why she had been stomping all over her neighbors' backyards, trampling all over their nice flower beds before returning home. It was another mystery that had baffled me, and that had now been solved. Mike knew about this, of course, but he didn't much care, as long as Mikaela didn't trample all over their own flower beds, which is why he'd planted plastic forks all around them. Partly to prevent cats and dogs from getting in there, but also to prevent his wife, who was always barefoot, from destroying them.

I eyed my friends keenly. I could see they were chewing on these solutions to the various mysteries I'd given them. And while they were thusly engaged, I tentatively put my head down for my long-overdue nap. But of course it was not to be, for Dooley suddenly gave me a sort of constipated look, and it was obvious that he was brooding on another question.

"Max?"

"Yes!"

"The turtles."

"What about them?"

"What's going to happen to them now that Mike is in jail?"

"They'll probably move to Florida with Mikaela," I said.

He smiled a happy smile. "Oh, good for them. They always wanted to move there, didn't they?"

"Yes, they did. And so did Mikaela. It was actually Mike who was desperate to move into the house that the Turners owned. Mikaela liked the place, but she could take it or leave it."

Which just goes to show that couples should probably communicate more. If Mikaela had told her husband loud and clear that she wanted to move to Florida, he might not have worked out that crazy plan of his. Then again, maybe they'd have selected a Florida dream home that had also been occupied by another couple, and he would have gone on a killing spree in Florida.

And since I could see that Dooley had more questions for me, and so did Harriet, Brutus, and even Mooch, I finally decided to make a break for it and more or less gracefully jumped down from that swing and waddled off as fast as my paws could carry me. My friends watched me go for a few moments, but then quickly recovered from their initial shock and hurried after me.

"Max!" Dooley yelled. "Where are you going?"

"Come back here, Max!" Harriet cried. "Come back here right now!"

"You can't outrun us, buddy!" Brutus cried. "We're faster than you!"

"I'm not," said Mooch. "But I'm going to give it my best shot anyway."

And so, while Tex was grilling meat and his family was enjoying their meal, our humans watched with not a small measure of surprise as one big blorange cat was chased around their backyard by three other cats and one dog. I can imagine we offered an entertaining spectacle, and judging by the merriment that rippled through the crowd, we gave good value for their money.

All I can say in my defense is that Hercule Poirot never had to go through this ordeal, nor did Sherlock Holmes or Miss Marple. But then they never had to contend with a trio of very persistent feline friends and one dog who didn't seem to understand one basic truth: all I want to do is nap!

THE END

Thanks for reading! If you want to know when a new Nic Saint book comes out, sign up for Nic's mailing list: nicsaint.com/news

EXCERPT FROM PURRFECT CHARADE (MAX 68)

Prologue

Jack Harper had been lying on his towel, minding his own business, when he was alerted to the presence of an interruption of the peace and quiet of his pool time by droplets of cold water sprinkling on his person. He opened his eyes but could only see that a person or persons unknown were blocking the sun. He tried to shield his eyes to take in this person but found it hard going. Finally, the person spoke, and as his eyes adjusted, he finally saw her steadily, and he saw her whole. She was a woman of considerably handsome aspect, and when she spoke, there was a lilt of something exotic in the way she formed the words.

"You're in my spot, mister," she said. The way she said it suggested that she didn't think it all that important that he move forthwith. More like amusement that he would have the sheer gall to occupy a spot that had clearly been assigned to her.

"I-I'm sorry," said Jack. "I didn't know."

EXCERPT FROM PURRFECT CHARADE (MAX 68)

"That's all right. I guess I could just as well take the spot next to you, Mr..."

"Harper," said Jack, mesmerized by the presence of such a gorgeous creature standing a mere foot away from him. "Jack Harper. And you are..."

"Madeline," said the woman, and proceeded to position herself on the sun lounger right next to his.

As they were pretty much the only people present at the pool at this early hour, there were plenty of spaces to choose from, which is why he hadn't really considered that any of these spots would have been reserved. As a cruise ship newbie, he was still trying to come to terms with the ins and outs of cruise ship traveling, and so if he stepped on a few toes from time to time, it wasn't out of malice but simply because he didn't know what the correct etiquette was.

"You a first-time traveler, Jack?" asked Madeline now as she languidly started applying what looked like sunscreen to her bronzed skin. It looked like satin, he decided. And for some reason, he felt a powerful urge to reach out and touch it. But of course, he refrained from doing so. He might be a cruise ship newbie, but at least he knew he shouldn't go about touching completely strange women. That kind of behavior might see him kicked off the boat, and then where would he be?

"Yeah, this is my first time traveling on the Ruritania, actually," he confessed. "Why? Is it that obvious?"

She laughed, a tinkling sort of laugh. "Yeah, pretty much," she said. "But you picked a great one for your first trip, Jack. The Ruritania is probably the best ship traveling the seven seas at the moment. Built in Germany, she's one of the highest quality and largest cruise liners ever built. And it shows."

"You seem to know a lot about cruise liners," he said

EXCERPT FROM PURRFECT CHARADE (MAX 68)

admiringly. "I take it this isn't your first time traveling on the Ruritania?"

"Oh, no, I've traveled on her loads of times. All the time, in fact." She gave him a radiant smile that could compete with the sun for first place in sheer radiance. "I live on board, you see. I'm part of the crew."

"Oh, you are? That's so great. So what do you do?" he asked, glad for this opportunity to have a chat with the woman before she turned away and disappeared into her own world, as most of the people on board seemed inclined to do. Since he was traveling alone, he had more or less hoped to strike up friendships with some of his fellow passengers, but so far, that hadn't happened yet, so this opportunity to engage someone in conversation was one he wasn't going to pass by.

"I'm the captain," said the woman simply, causing him to goggle at her to some extent. In his mind, captains were these gray-bearded distinguished older men who stood erect and tall and had a sort of iron grip and a look of steel in their icy blue eyes. But this epitome of loveliness looked probably as far removed from the typical image he had of a captain as he could have imagined.

"Your mouth is hanging open, Jack," said Madeline, looking amused.

"I... I'm sorry," he said. "It's just that... I mean you... I mean to say..."

"You don't think a woman can be the captain of a cruise ship?" she asked sweetly. "Is that it?"

"Oh, no!" he hastened to say. "Of course not. It's just that..." He finally gave up. It was probably obvious that he was both baffled and deeply impressed by this revelation.

"There are lots of women captains now," she said. "So you better get used to the idea, Jack. At least if you plan to become a regular cruise ship traveler. And now if you'll excuse me, I'm going to lie here for ten minutes and work on my tan. As you can imagine, captains of cruise vessels don't get a lot of time off, so I was actually hoping to make the most of my off-time."

And with these words, she closed her eyes, and it was clear that their conversation time had come to an end. At least for now. Jack lay back on his sun lounger, but try as he might, he couldn't quite see himself capable of relaxing after the startling revelation that the most gorgeous creature that he'd ever met—the woman lying right next to him, in fact—was also by way of being in charge of this entire vessel. It certainly put a very interesting spin on things, and as he gave himself up to thought, he wondered if he should have told her about the reason he was on board the Ruritania. If he had, she might not have smiled at him with such radiance or talked to him with such enjoyment.

No, if she really knew what he was doing on board her boat, she probably would have had him arrested on the spot and locked him up below decks in one of the brigs. Then again, nothing ventured, nothing gained, and so he decided to take a leap of faith.

Chapter One

Vesta Muffin and her friend Scarlett Canyon hurried to their designated spot at the pool. After having spent a couple of days aboard the Ruritania, they were slowly starting to become acquainted with the habits and the mores on board the vessel. For one thing, if you wanted to have a great spot by the pool, you had to hurry and make sure you beat the other passengers to it. And since some of these passengers were perfectly ready, willing, and also able to kick you in the shins if they thought that would suit their purpose, it was paramount to develop a strategy. And so, along with Scarlett, she had devised just such a method of securing the best spot. It was all about the wrists, she knew. You had to race to the sun loungers from the moment the pool deck was being opened for the day, then flick your towel from afar and cause it to land in the right spot. For the moment your towel had landed on the sun lounger, that lounger was officially yours, and nobody could touch it. It took some doing, and she and Scarlett had spent the better part of their second day on board practicing their throwing technique, but now they were experts, and Scarlett was even better at it than Vesta was. She could throw a mean towel from no less than twenty feet away, beating all the other contestants of the daily race and thus securing herself the perfect spot by the main pool.

It was just one of those things that the travel agency hadn't mentioned in the glossy brochures these companies like to publish, extolling the many advantages and virtues of traveling aboard the cruise line's flagship, the Ruritania, but it was one the two friends had learned in record time.

The same thing applied to breakfast, of course. Even though the crew prided itself on making sure that all passengers were always fed and the breakfast buffet was supplied on a continuous basis during official breakfast hours, Vesta had discovered that if you arrived even half an hour late, a lot of the good stuff was gone, and the buffet looked as if a horde of ravenous wild beasts had attacked it and left nothing but crumbs for those who came behind. So it was important that you lined up in front of the restaurant twenty minutes before the doors were officially opened, and used your elbows to muscle to the front of the line and get in there first. She knew what she wanted, and so did Scarlett, and so the moment they burst through those doors, they were already making a beeline for the sushi rolls filled with raw fish and avocado, getting in there before the vultures arrived.

EXCERPT FROM PURRFECT CHARADE (MAX 68)

Others might have said it was a stressful way to start the day, but not for Vesta and Scarlett. It was simply part and parcel of traveling with hundreds or possibly even thousands of other passengers on the same boat. And since they were determined to make the most of their time on the ship, the strategy the two friends had devised suited them perfectly. The only thing they hadn't managed yet was to secure themselves a seat at the captain's table. But they had plans in that regard. Big plans, and they were determined to see them through. Before their voyage was over, Vesta and Scarlett would become the captain's new best friends, even if the man didn't know it yet.

Vesta had seen the captain, and she had decided that he was going to become her second husband, or conversely, Scarlett's first. Handsome as could be, with a distinguished white beard and those cool blue eyes that set him apart from all the other males of the species, she knew that wedding bells would ring out in her near future. But since Scarlett had confessed to her that she had also heard those very same wedding bells ring in her ears, Vesta was quite willing to forgo the big prize and become Scarlett's maid of honor if that's how the dice rolled. But until then, it was every woman for herself, and if Scarlett didn't make a move, she most certainly would.

"Oh, isn't he just the most gorgeous man you have ever seen?" she asked now as she smeared a liberal amount of sunscreen on her chest. "He's just so... captainy, isn't he?"

"He is very captainy," said Scarlett. "But something tells me that we're not the only ones in the running for the big prize, honey." She gestured with her head to the captain as he lay next to a woman of bronzed and exotic aspect, who was amiably chatting with the captain. And if Vesta's eyes weren't deceiving her, the captain wasn't fully impervious to the devious vixen's charms either, as he was grinning like a moron while he listened to whatever the woman was pouring into his ear.

Vesta's face clouded. "Treacherous little minx," she muttered under her breath. "You see that all the time, don't you? Women throwing themselves at the captain like that. Making a total fool of themselves." She could have added that she was just such a woman, and in all likelihood, so was Scarlett. But then they had both determined that the captain was theirs for the taking, and so by all rights he shouldn't engage this other woman in conversation and revel in the dubious privilege.

"She's pretty," said Scarlett, and if Vesta wasn't mistaken, there was a touch of jealousy in her voice.

"I guess so," said Vesta reluctantly. "If you like the type."

"The captain certainly likes the type," said Scarlett.

And as they watched on, the conversation between the two seemed to have come to an end, and they both lay back on their respective sun loungers and closed their eyes. Clearly, the captain had decided that enough was enough and had told the woman in no uncertain terms what he thought of passengers becoming entirely too fresh with him.

Vesta relaxed. And as she started thinking up ways and means of approaching the man and snagging his attention, she knew she was in for a tough time since she was obviously facing stiff competition. But she was nothing if not determined and knew that she would come out the victor in this ruthless campaign she was about to engage in. A captain's wife. Now wouldn't that be something? Then she could move out of her daughter's place and travel the seven seas by the side of her handsome captain, being awarded all the perks that probably went with the position. For one thing, she would never have to struggle to get first dibs on a sun lounger in the morning ever again, for the captain's wife probably had her very own lounger reserved especially for her. Maybe even her own private deck with her own private pool. And she would get the best food at the breakfast buffet, the best cabin, and the best service supplied to her free of charge. And as she freely indulged in her daydream of the kind of glorious life she would lead once she became the Ruritania's First Lady, she didn't notice that a hidden hand had snuck up behind her, grabbed the bag she had brought along that contained her wallet and her phone, then retracted again, removing the items and securing them for its own. The same procedure was repeated seconds later with Scarlett's bag and about a dozen other passengers all enjoying those first rays of sun heating up the pool deck. It was a nice haul, and all perpetrated under the nose of the ship's actual captain, who wasn't the gray-haired man who answered to the name Jack Harper but the woman lying next to him.

Chapter Two

Marge wasn't all that keen on the fact that their cruise wasn't going to take them to the one island she had been looking forward to visiting. It had been on the itinerary when they set out on this journey, but apparently something had gone wrong, and now all of a sudden it wasn't on the schedule anymore. It was a small island in the Caribbean, and she had read great things about it, both about the local population's hospitality and friendliness, but also about the springs located in one of the island's spas, which were supposed to possess rejuvenating qualities and be able tc cure any diseases you might be suffering from. And since she had been experiencing a slight pain in her right hand lately, she had been hoping that bathing in that healing spring water, which allegedly sprang up straight from the Earth's core, might alleviate the malady she had.

As it was, her husband of twenty-five years, who was a doctor himself, had told her it was all hogwash, and she shouldn't give credence to a bunch of nonsense stories and local hoodoo. Just a way to fleece the tourists, he had said. If she gave into that sort of thing, she was simply perpetuating a myth and allowing these crooks to continue swindling naive people.

Still, when she read on that day's schedule that the trip to the island had been canceled and the boat would steam ahead to their next destination, she felt a distinct pang of regret. The pain in her hand was one thing, but her granddaughter Grace had developed a sort of skin rash lately on her upper back, and she just knew that a dip in that healing spring water would have cleared it right up.

"I don't understand," she told her daughter while the family was enjoying a nice breakfast. "Why did they decide to skip a trip to Marker Island?"

"Probably because King Kong has been spotted," her husband said in a weak attempt at humor.

She made a face at him. "It's not funny, Tex. I was really looking forward to visiting those springs. They're world-famous, and on TripAdvisor there are lots and lots of very positive comments. Hundreds of them, in fact. It would have cleared up Grace's rash."

Odelia gave her a look of commiseration. "Maybe you can ask the captain?" she suggested. "There must be a reason they decided to change the itinerary. Though if you're worried about Grace's rash, don't be. It's practically gone already, with that new cream Dad prescribed."

"They're probably behind schedule," said Chase, Marge's son-in-law. "So they figured they'd better make up for lost time by skipping a destination or two. It happens."

Chase and Odelia were experienced cruise ship travelers, Marge knew. They had done a cruise for their honeymoon,

EXCERPT FROM PURRFECT CHARADE (MAX 68)

taking along their cats for that occasion, or at least two of them. This time, to celebrate Tex and Marge's twenty-fifth wedding anniversary, the rest of the family had all chipped in and decided to offer the happy couple a Caribbean cruise, something Marge had been dreaming of for years but which had never materialized. But now it was finally happening.

"I'm sure there will be springs on other islands," said Tex now, giving her a rub across the back. "And if you really want to pay a visit to this particular island, we could always come back next year and do it all over again."

She gave him a grateful look. She knew it probably wouldn't happen, but then again, it might. So she decided to put the whole Marker Island business out of her head and focus on the bright side, which was that she was there with her family, and they were having a great time.

"Where is Gran?" asked Odelia now, looking around. "She wasn't in her cabin when I knocked on the door just now to tell her we were heading out."

"She and Scarlett are lounging by the pool," said Tex. "They got up early again so they could get first dibs on the best spots by the pool and also be the first at the breakfast buffet." He shook his head. "They seem to believe that if you're not first to attack the buffet, there will be nothing left."

"Well, it is true that some food items already seem to be finished," said Odelia as she took a bite from her pancake.

"I thought they kept refreshing all morning," said Marge.

"That's the idea," said Tex. "But sometimes they run out of stuff before everyone has had a chance to sample all the items on display, so they simply move some of the other stuff around so it doesn't look obvious things have run out. Which is something Vesta seems to know very well."

Vesta and Scarlett had quickly become experts at this cruise liner thing, and it was obvious that the two older ladies were having a whale of a time. First dibs on the breakfast buffet, first dibs on the best spots by the pool. And their next plan was to get first dibs on a seat at the captain's table for dinner. So far, that particular honor had escaped them, but Marge was convinced it wouldn't be long before they were glued to the captain and wouldn't let go until the man had promised either of the two friends to marry them.

"They certainly have taken to cruise life like a fish to water," said Chase with a grin.

"They've been looking forward to this cruise so much," said Marge. "They've been reading everything they could lay their hands on and watching documentaries, YouTube videos, and movies about cruise life for months now."

"If I didn't know any better," said Tex, "they might even consider becoming fixtures on the Ruritania." A sort of wistful look had come into his eyes, and Marge knew what he was thinking. If he could unload his mother-in-law onto the cruise line company, it would probably be the best day of his life. But since Ma was one of those people who are an acquired taste, Marge didn't think that would happen. They would simply return her to sender as soon as possible.

She glanced around, and when she saw that their four cats were seated next to the table and snacking from their bowls, she relaxed. She hadn't thought they'd be allowed to bring their cats on board. Pet dogs, yes, by all means, but pet cats? She didn't think she had ever heard of people taking a trip aboard a cruise ship with their cats in tow, but the Ruritania was one of the only cruise liners that allowed pets on board, so they had applied for and received permission to do just that, and so now Max, Dooley, Brutus, and Harriet were all aboard, and even though they were still getting used to it, they didn't seem to be overly put out by the sudden shift of environment.

She picked up the remnants of her soft-boiled egg and

EXCERPT FROM PURRFECT CHARADE (MAX 68)

deposited it onto Max's plate. She watched with interest how he discarded the white and concentrated on the yolk for some reason. He ate it all, then proceeded to start licking himself, blithely ignoring his benefactor, as most cats do.

She shared a look of amusement with her daughter, who had been watching.

Cats. They love you when they need something, then when they get it, they simply ignore you.

Suddenly there was a sort of commotion near the entrance to the restaurant, which was one of many different restaurants on board the gigantic vessel but had quickly become their favorite. When Marge looked up, she saw that her mother and Scarlett were approaching, and they didn't look happy. Both ladies were dressed in their bathing suits, which wasn't allowed in the restaurant, something the hostess at the entrance of the restaurant was pointing out to them. But Ma being Ma, she simply ignored the woman and steamed on the moment she caught sight of her family.

"We've been robbed!" she shouted from thirty yards away. "Someone stole our phones and our wallets!"

"Oh, Christ," said Chase under his breath.

"And we weren't the only ones," Scarlett added. "At least a dozen people lost their personal possessions, some of them their passports and other valuables!"

"And we tried to complain to the captain, but he said he's not the captain at all!" said Ma and seemed even more aggrieved by this betrayal of her confidence than the actual theft of her stuff.

"What do you mean, the captain isn't the captain?" asked Odelia.

"Just what I'm telling you: we told the captain about our stuff being stolen, and the man had the sheer audacity to claim that he wasn't the captain! Probably trying to shirk his duty!"

EXCERPT FROM PURRFECT CHARADE (MAX 68)

"You do know that the captain of the Ruritania is a woman, right?" said Odelia.

The look on both Ma and Scarlett's faces was something to behold.

"A woman!" Ma cried, much aggrieved. "But why?!"

"Because women can captain a boat just as well as men can," Odelia pointed out. "So the man you thought was the captain is probably just another passenger, just like us."

"But... but... but..." Ma sputtered, looking like a kid whose candy had been taken away. "But that's not fair!"

"I get first dibs on the passenger," Scarlett said quickly. And when her friend eyed her in abject dismay, she shrugged. "He may not be the captain, but he's still a very handsome man, honey."

Ma threw up her hands. "This cruise is going to hell in a handbasket!" she yelled, and then she pointed a finger at Chase, for some reason. "You have to find our stuff and arrest this thief, Chase."

"Why me?!" Chase cried.

"Because you're a cop, and it's your duty to do... cop stuff."

"I'm on vacation!" said Chase. "And besides, I don't have any jurisdiction here. Go talk to the captain. The actual captain this time, not some passenger who looks like a captain. He'll probably refer you to the ship's security team, and they'll take your statements and catch this thief."

But Ma wasn't so easily appeased. "I don't trust this captain," she said.

"Why?" asked Odelia. "Because she's a woman?"

"Because she's been cheating us! Making us believe this other guy is the captain."

It was the kind of specious logic Marge's mother excelled at. Only this time she was about to be put in her place, Marge saw, for the actual captain had appeared at their table. She was a woman of Marge's age, with red hair tied back in a ponytail and perfectly attired in a captain's uniform. She gave Ma a look of censure. But when she opened her mouth to speak, she was nothing if not perfectly civil and professional. "The deck steward has informed me about the thefts," she told them. "And I want to apologize on behalf of the crew and tell you that we will do everything in our power to make sure it doesn't happen again and that the thief will be apprehended, and your property returned."

"You shouldn't have put this other guy in charge," said Ma.

The captain gave her a look of confusion. "You mean the deck steward?"

"No, the other captain! When we told him what happened, he said he wasn't the captain, and I don't think it's fair."

The captain simply stared at her and gave her a look that Marge had become quite accustomed to over the years. It was the kind of look a lot of people gave Ma Muffin when she was going well. "I don't understand," she finally confessed.

"Don't listen to her," Tex advised since he never did so himself. "She's had a big shock."

The captain's expression instantly morphed into one of compassion. "Of course you have. And like I said, we'll catch the person responsible and return the stolen items as soon as possible. In the meantime, we would like to offer you free drinks for the rest of your trip, and that goes for your entire party." She made a gesture encompassing all those present at the table, and Marge gave the woman a look of approval. Free drinks all around were a nice way to compensate them for the trouble this thief had caused.

But of course, Ma wouldn't have it. "Who cares about free drinks?" she asked. "You should never have allowed this thief to come on board in the first place. So what you're going to do is hire my granddaughter and her husband, and they'll make sure this never happens again."

"I'm sorry, your granddaughter and her husband?" asked the captain.

"They're cops," said Ma proudly. "And they've solved a lot of cases back home. In fact, they never fail at any task they set themselves, so if you add them to your personnel roster, you can be safe in the knowledge that this thief is as good as caught." And when the captain opened her mouth to speak, Ma waved a hand. "You don't have to thank me. It's the least I can do. And now I would like you to introduce Scarlett to your captain who isn't a captain because she's got first dibs, and even though I like the guy myself, Scarlett is my best friend, and if she wants to marry this guy, I'm not going to stand in the way of her future happiness. So lead the way, my dear, and we will follow."

The captain closed her mouth again, and if the dazed look in her eyes was any indication, she was probably already regretting that she had ever welcomed Vesta Muffin aboard the Ruritania in the first place. But then she wasn't the first, and probably wouldn't be the last, to have a feeling of being sandbagged after making Marge's mom's acquaintance. She often had that effect on people.

ABOUT NIC

Nic has a background in political science and before being struck by the writing bug worked odd jobs around the world (including but not limited to massage therapist in Mexico, gardener in Italy, restaurant manager in India, and Berlitz teacher in Belgium).

When he's not writing he enjoys curling up with a good (comic) book, watching British crime dramas, French comedies or Nancy Meyers movies, sampling pastry (apple cake!), pasta and chocolate (preferably the dark variety), twisting himself into a pretzel doing morning yoga, going for a run, and spoiling his big red tomcat Tommy.

He lives with his wife (and aforementioned cat) in a small village smack dab in the middle of absolutely nowhere and is probably writing his next 'Mysteries of Max' book right now.

www.nicsaint.com

ALSO BY NIC SAINT

The Mysteries of Max
Purrfect Murder
Purrfectly Deadly
Purrfect Revenge
Purrfect Heat
Purrfect Crime
Purrfect Rivalry
Purrfect Peril
Purrfect Secret
Purrfect Alibi
Purrfect Obsession
Purrfect Betrayal
Purrfectly Clueless
Purrfectly Royal
Purrfect Cut
Purrfect Trap
Purrfectly Hidden
Purrfect Kill
Purrfect Boy Toy
Purrfectly Dogged
Purrfectly Dead
Purrfect Saint
Purrfect Advice
Purrfect Passion

A Purrfect Gnomeful
Purrfect Cover
Purrfect Patsy
Purrfect Son
Purrfect Fool
Purrfect Fitness
Purrfect Setup
Purrfect Sidekick
Purrfect Deceit
Purrfect Ruse
Purrfect Swing
Purrfect Cruise
Purrfect Harmony
Purrfect Sparkle
Purrfect Cure
Purrfect Cheat
Purrfect Catch
Purrfect Design
Purrfect Life
Purrfect Thief
Purrfect Crust
Purrfect Bachelor
Purrfect Double
Purrfect Date
Purrfect Hit
Purrfect Baby
Purrfect Mess
Purrfect Paris

Purrfect Model

Purrfect Slug

Purrfect Match

Purrfect Game

Purrfect Bouquet

Purrfect Home

Purrfectly Slim

Purrfect Nap

Purrfect Yacht

Purrfect Scam

Purrfect Fury

Purrfect Christmas

Purrfect Gems

Purrfect Demons

Purrfect Show

Purrfect Impasse

The Mysteries of Max Collections

Collection 1 (Books 1-3)

Collection 2 (Books 4-6)

Collection 3 (Books 7-9)

Collection 4 (Books 10-12)

Collection 5 (Books 13-15)

Collection 6 (Books 16-18)

Collection 7 (Books 19-21)

Collection 8 (Books 22-24)

Collection 9 (Books 25-27)

Collection 10 (Books 28-30)

Collection 11 (Books 31-33)

Collection 12 (Books 34-36)
Collection 13 (Books 37-39)
Collection 14 (Books 40-42)
Collection 15 (Books 43-45)
Collection 16 (Books 46-48)
Collection 17 (Books 49-51)
Collection 18 (Books 52-54)
Collection 19 (Books 55-57)
Collection 20 (Books 58-60)
Collection 21 (Books 61-63)
Collection 22 (Books 64-66)

The Mysteries of Max Big Collections

Big Collection 1 (Books 1-10)
Big Collection 2 (Books 11-20)

The Mysteries of Max Short Stories

Collection 1 (Stories 1-3)
Collection 2 (Stories 4-7)

Nora Steel

Murder Retreat

The Kellys

Murder Motel
Death in Suburbia

Emily Stone

Murder at the Art Class

Washington & Jefferson

First Shot

Alice Whitehouse
Spooky Times
Spooky Trills
Spooky End
Spooky Spells

Ghosts of London
Between a Ghost and a Spooky Place
Public Ghost Number One
Ghost Save the Queen
Box Set 1 (Books 1-3)
A Tale of Two Harrys
Ghost of Girlband Past
Ghostlier Things

Charleneland
Deadly Ride
Final Ride

Neighborhood Witch Committee
Witchy Start
Witchy Worries
Witchy Wishes

Saffron Diffley
Crime and Retribution
Vice and Verdict
Felonies and Penalties (Saffron Diffley Short 1)

The B-Team
Once Upon a Spy

Tate-à-Tate
Enemy of the Tates

Ghosts vs. Spies
The Ghost Who Came in from the Cold

Witchy Fingers
Witchy Trouble
Witchy Hexations
Witchy Possessions
Witchy Riches
Box Set 1 (Books 1-4)

The Mysteries of Bell & Whitehouse
One Spoonful of Trouble
Two Scoops of Murder
Three Shots of Disaster
Box Set 1 (Books 1-3)
A Twist of Wraith
A Touch of Ghost
A Clash of Spooks
Box Set 2 (Books 4-6)
The Stuffing of Nightmares
A Breath of Dead Air
An Act of Hodd
Box Set 3 (Books 7-9)
A Game of Dons

Standalone Novels

When in Bruges

The Whiskered Spy

ThrillFix

Homejacking

The Eighth Billionaire

The Wrong Woman